TYPICAL
Chi Sh*t

TYPICAL
Chi Sh*t

Sassy Silverman

SASSY WORLD LLC
Chicago, IL

TYPICAL CHI SH*T

This book is a work of fiction. Names, characters, places, and incidents are the product of the author's imagination or are used fictitiously. Any resemblance to actual events, locales, or persons, living or dead, is strictly coincidental.

TYPICAL CHI SH*T © Dominique Taylor

All rights reserved. No part of this publication may be recorded, stored in a retrieval system, or transmitted in any form or by any means, electronic, mechanical, photocopying, recording, or otherwise, without prior written permission from the publisher.

Paperback ISBN: 978-0-578-87726-6

Published by Sassy World LLC
Chicago, IL

Printed in the United States of America
First Edition April 2021

Cover Design by: Make Your Mark Publishing Solutions
Interior Layout by: Make Your Mark Publishing Solutions
Editing: Make Your Mark Publishing Solutions

ACKNOWLEDGEMENTS

I WOULD LIKE to thank Monique from Make Your Mark Publishing Solutions for leading, guiding, and teaching me throughout this process. I couldn't have done this without you.

This book is dedicated to my daughter, Destiny Silverman. My dream when I was sixteen years old was to write and publish books. I never gave up on that dream, and now that it has happened at age thirty-five, I want you to know that no matter what you do in life, never give up and always follow your dreams.

CHAPTER 1

"WOW!" DAVID SAID in a shaky voice while looking at me all dressed up for his high school graduation. These past two months, I just been lounging around, not getting dressed at all. As I bent over, adjusting my red platform Louboutins, his eyes were glued to me. The shoes went perfectly with my white bodycon dress. The dress had my 130 pounds looking real thick. Thanks to my extra four inches, for once, I stood taller than David. Without the pumps, I was only five feet tall. I was thick in all the right places, which was my ass and thighs. My stomach was ironing-board flat. My beautiful golden-brown skin shone bright from the last-minute facial by my home girl, SkinByLyn. I was determined to walk into graduation stealing all the attention.

I should've been graduating with my best friends today,

but I just couldn't pull myself together because of the brutal murder of my mother exactly sixty-one days ago.

David tried preaching for me to finish, but that only led to arguments. David had always been a good friend, but these last few months, he was everything I needed. We built an unbreakable bond. He put up with my mood swings, drunken nights, and bossy ways. As much as I wanted to miss his graduation because of the embarrassment of not walking across the stage, I knew I couldn't.

David and I had been inseperable since third grade. We were next-door neighbors for a year, and our moms were the best of friends. Then, eventually, my dad kept his promises and got us out the hood. I practically had a fit when my mother tried to switch my school. My mom preached that I would get a better education in our new neighborhood. After I cried to my dad for hours, he gave in and demanded I stay at Burke Elementary with my two best friends: David and Britt. I loved that I always got my way with my dad after a few tears.

My dad was my best friend. When he died of a heart attack, it almost killed me. The day I found out that my dad would no longer walk through our doors late at night and kiss me on the forehead, sneak money under my pillow, or always override my mother's decisions, I lost it. I did exactly what I had seen on Lifetime movies—I tried to kill myself. I took a bunch of pain pills and thought that it would end my life, but it just embarrassed me and I was known as the suicidal kid at school. That was the beginning of David and Britt having my back.

Britt was a firecracker. She dared a person to come at me with bullshit; she was always ready to fight any chick that stepped up. David handled all the guys. Sometimes he was a bit overprotective as if he were my dad, but I admired him for that. And that's why I put all my fears under the table to be at their graduation.

Time was moving fast, and although it was only 10:00 a.m. I had the smell of yak on my breath. I placed a piece of watermelon-flavored bubblegum in my mouth for now, but the mixture of Hennessy and orange juice sat inside my cup with a few cubes of ice, ready for my ride to this graduation. I knew drinking was bad, but it was all I had to help with the pain of losing my mother.

"Damn, David, you looking good!" I said as David turned the corner of the kitchen dressed in his all-white suit, looking like Will Smith from a *Bay Boys* scene.

David was tall at six foot two, and he was ripped. His chest and stomach were full of muscles. He had a chestnut skin complexion with the cutest hazel eyes. He definitely grew from the chubby boy that I had met in the third grade. David wore a Mohawk haircut, but not the kind of Mohawk you would see on a rockstar. His hair was tapered around the sides and was very curly. He constantly walked around with his hair sponge, making sure his curls were tight. I loved fiddling through his curls every night while we chilled. He was every girl's crush, and I had the luxury of being his best friend.

"Jaz, let's go. Grab your coffee or whatever that is so we won't be late," David said, giving me the side eye. I guess I wasn't doing a good job of hiding the liquor smell. I couldn't fake it. I did the walk of shame as I passed him as he held the door open for me. I thought, *I'm grown and I shouldn't have to hide my habit from David or no one else.* High school diploma or not, I was almost nineteen years old with my own everything, thanks to my parents. My mom left me her business, along with a nice insurance policy. I didn't want for anything

As we arrived at the school, David rushed out the car to go line up with the other graduates. I never imagined walking through those high school doors again. I made my mind up over a month ago about school, right around finals. I had several teachers reaching out to me, but I refused to take the last few tests that would have allowed me to walk across the stage.

I sat for about five minutes in my car, trying to down as much of my drink as I could. Dropping out of school was more depressing than my first suicide attempt. There I was, finally out my car and walking slowly through the hallways—the same hallway where I had lounged by the lockers, staring at boys with Britt, and the same hallway where I had my first kiss with Mike. Ugh, just the thought of Mike's damn name had me teary-eyed, thinking of how he was part of the setup that got my mom robbed and killed.

It wasn't long before I entered the auditorium. My head had to be high, so I wiped my face and walked through those doors as if I were a graduate myself.

"Jaz, over here!" David's little sisters were screaming across the room.

David's mom had saved me a seat right next to them. As I sat down, I slipped on big, dark shades to hide my red eyes. I was sure they were red as hell because I had smoked three blunts before coming to this damn graduation: one when I first opened my eyes this morning, one while getting dressed, and my last one in the car headed to this damn place. I needed to be relaxed and not on edge just in case a muthafucka had some smart shit to say because I'd already beat three bitches down this month. My attitude was reckless, and I didn't care because I didn't have shit else to lose at this point.

I was looking down the entire time to avoid eye contact with any teachers who would look my way, but when I lifted my head, I couldn't believe who I saw. Detective Williams. I had only seen the detective two times: once when he was picking me up from lying over my mother's dead body, and another time when he was picking me up from stomping the shit out of my mother's friend, who had something to do with her murder. I remember him so well because both times, he was gentle with me.

I remember the night of my mom's murder. I walked up and saw half her body in the salon and the other half out, covered in blood.

I ran toward her body and Detective Williams tried to hold me, but I broke loose, falling onto the ground next to her, kneeling in her puddle of blood. I touched her face; it was still slightly warm. She lay there, lifeless, her almond eyes forever closed, her full lips clamped shut. If it wasn't for the blood, I would've thought she was sleeping.

My chest was burning. My face was on my mother's face. "Wake up, Mama," I cried. "Wake up, Ma. We got to go home."

I tried to grab her arm. I just wanted her to get up and come home with me. Detective Williams lifted me. I tried to break loose to get back on the floor with my mom; I couldn't dare leave her on that cold marble floor alone, but Detective Williams held me close to his chest, asking me to stay calm. That night was the worst night of my life, and just sitting there thinking of it made my eyes fill with water. I tried to catch my tears before they fell down my face because the last thing I wanted was sympathy at this graduation.

I locked eyes with Detective Williams again and he waved at me with the biggest smile. I gave him a quick wave in response and looked back down. This was my first time seeing him and how good he really looked. He was dark, tall, and bald, and his melanin was popping so good that I couldn't figure out his exact age. Detective Williams was already fully established in his career, so I knew he was a lot older than me. I hoped not old enough to be having a child graduating today because I would feel sick to my stomach drooling over one of my classmates' dads.

"David Shepherd," the announcer called.

"Yay! David, that's my boy!" David's mom yelled while his sisters and I clapped and chanted, "David! David! David!"

Brittany Staples was called after David. I was already on my feet and yelling my girl's name. I was proud of her because Britt glided right through high school with her Cs and Ds.

It felt like two hours passed, but once the graduation was finally over, I sprinted toward the door.

I heard, "Hey, Jaz, nice to see you." I turned around to find Detective Williams standing there.

"Nice to see you too," I mumbled.

"Why don't I see your name on the program?" he asked.

"Why are you looking for my name?" I sassed, slightly tipsy. He was being a bit nosy.

"Sorry if I'm overstepping."

"You are," I said, pushing the sunglasses on my face and attempting to walk off.

"Are you ready, Uncle?" asked a young girl who resembled him.

"Well, nice seeing you, Jaz."

"Likewise," I said, practically running out the door.

I rushed to my car, praying that I left a sip in my cup before I got out. The graduation, the detective, and the thoughts of my mother were too much … I needed something fast to release my mind. I sat in the car, digging through my purse, trying to see if I had half of a Perc. I wanted to be lifted before David got back in the car.

"Damn!" I screamed as David scared me by knocking on the driver's side window. I was so focused in my purse that I didn't see him walk up.

"My bad, Jaz. I was just letting you know I'm riding with my mom, so just follow us," David said with the biggest smile. He was so happy about this day.

"Cool," I said, smiling back on the outside but feeling miserable on the inside.

I followed David, his mom, and his sisters to a buffet. Over the last few months, I had gotten very close to David's mom. She was always good to talk to. David and I also grew closer, and I mean that in the nastiest way. David and I were best friends, but somehow after my mom passed, we found our way in the sheets. Maybe it was all the hanging out and drinking that I was doing. David would occasionally drink, but most nights he would just watch me throw back shots. I had never had sex before, and I couldn't think of a more perfect person to lose my virginity to.

The first time was during Netflix-and-chill—then Netflix-and-chill turned into sex and sleep. I made the first move during David's speech about how I needed to slow down drinking and finish school. In the middle of him talking, I made up my mind about what I wanted, so I just went for it. I got up and sat on his lap while putting my tongue in his mouth to make sure he couldn't say shit else. I didn't stop and he didn't either. He slowly put his hand under my gown and slipped his fingers inside me.

"Are you sure about this? Do you want me to stop?" he whispered several times between kisses.

Each time, I shook my head, encouraging him to continue. His fingers slowly stroked the inside of me and it felt good. Every time I moaned, he kissed my open mouth. I reached to grab his dick, rubbing it until it was rock solid. David climbed on top of me, our lips touching and our eyes locked on each other, then ... OMG! There it was—his dick inside of me. I moaned loud as hell, and I was embarrassed until ... soon after, he bust. Yep, that's right; after all the years I'd anticipated sex, and it was over in five minutes.

David explained, "Damn, that pussy was tight!"

I just looked at him. I didn't know what to say. He never moved from inside me; he lay there, right on my chest, and fell asleep. Those few little strokes did feel good. It wasn't long-lasting sex like I'd seen in movies, but at least it was with someone I trusted.

Those Henny shots that night had me spinning. I couldn't sleep, so I lay there in deep thought. I couldn't believe I lost my virginity to my best friend. A thousand questions raced through my head. *Is he my man now? Will we still be best friends? Will he tell the entire school?* My head and body were feeling two different things. My body was relaxed, but my brain was a wreck. My feelings had shifted. I couldn't stop thinking about my mom, but now I was thinking about the sex too.

I hated that it happened during this fucked-up time in my life, but in a weird way, I felt I needed it. Although David and I had been best friends since the third grade, I always imagined my first time being with him. Unlike me, he had a lot of experience. He'd been telling me his sex stories for years. This muthafucka started at twelve years old!

Casual sex between us had been going on for a few weeks. We never talked about being an official couple, and we hadn't told anyone about the sex—not even Britt. She had been pressuring me about my virginity ever since she lost hers back in seventh grade.

At the dinner table, David's mom was staring at me. Every time I looked up from my plate, she was all in my damn face. She smiled.

"Jaz, thank you for keeping David on track with school all these years. I know you did most of his homework since I never saw him with a pen or paper at home."

I looked at David; he looked at the ceiling. His mother was right. I had done all his work up until two months before graduation.

"What am I going to do without you in college?" David asked.

"Fail," one of his little sisters blurted out.

We all started to laugh at his sister's joke, and it was perfect timing because I didn't want to be pressured about school anymore. Besides that, we had a party to go to after dinner. It was time to turn up.

The party at Monica's house was lit as fuck. Monica was the *grown* girl at school. She was more advanced than most of us girls. She'd been wearing blinged-out nails since we were in seventh grade, and her parents let her do anything she wanted. The rest of us were grateful because we were always lit at her house.

As I sipped my much-needed yak, I noticed that Monica was all over David. I couldn't say a word since David and I weren't official, but I was livid. David must have felt the heat from my eyes because he kept pushing her off. But she was aggressive with it, and the more I sipped, the more I felt like a raging bull on the inside.

Britt walked up and, as she poured more Henny in my cup, said, "Bitch, what is wrong with you?"

"Nothing, G. I'm fine."

"Nah, bitch, you lyin'. I know that face from anywhere. You mad? That's your jealous look," she said while looking around.

"What are you talking about, Britt? I'm not mad."

"Oh, bitch, let me find out that David over there giving you more than moral support," she joked.

"Girl, shut up. Where the weed at?" I said, knowing if we got high, her mind would be off what David and I got going on and my mind would be in the clouds.

Although Britt was my bestie, she couldn't hold water, so I absolutely would not trust her with anything I wanted to keep private. With David's popularity at school, I know she would run and tell everybody that David and I were fucking.

My mom always said, "Never tell a muthafucka what's in your bank account or who you fucking. That type of shit ruins friendships quick."

Britt pulled out one of her skimpy-ass blunts, and we lit that muthafucka right up in the middle of the dance floor. David was finally able to break from Monica and came back to us with more shots of Hennessy. Boy, did I need it.

"I'm going to fuck the shit out of you when we get back to your house," David whispered in my ear.

I giggled, feeling turned on by those few words. I looked around and more people were coming in the door as if the party was just getting started. But I was ready to go. We stayed a little bit longer, turning the entire party out, dancing, smoking, and taking shots.

"Oh four!" the people chanted—the year that high school was finally over.

The entire house was celebrating graduation night, and although I didn't graduate, I felt the need to celebrate my new life as a boss bitch in charge.

CHAPTER 2

I WAS EMBARRASSED at how loud David was when we entered the lobby of my new condo. I had only been living there two weeks. "Aye, aye, I'm in love with a lit bitch," David rapped. He was so loud that the overnight doorman stood up and looked at us. I covered David's mouth all the way to the elevator so he couldn't say shit else. It felt weird watching someone else drunk for a change, but I couldn't judge David because most nights he was picking me up off the floor. When we reached the twenty-first floor, David stumbled off the elevator, almost falling to the ground. He was actually blowing my buzz.

As soon as I opened the door, David fell right on the couch. I left him there, hoping he would fall sound asleep. As I stared out the window, I felt blessed to have a view like this.

It had been so emotional living at my mom's house without her; the memories of her ate me up most nights. I barely got a full night of rest. I didn't sleep much at my new place, but it was peaceful looking at the water from my twenty-first-floor balcony. I was thankful for David's mom, who helped me get all my finances in order, including buying this condo. She guided me to the right people so I could put my mother's house for sale. Although my mother was gone, I did have a few people in my corner looking out for me.

I couldn't see the water outside in the dark, but I knew it was there. That's how I felt about my parents; I couldn't physically see them in my life, but I knew they were there spiritually. After ten minutes, I decided to go take a warm shower. David was snoring, and I knew he was in a deep sleep by now. With so many emotions running through my mind, it was time to tune out. I played some '90s R&B in the bathroom, setting the mood right before I jumped in the shower.

The mood was relaxing and the water was running over my body. Suddenly, I felt a waft of cold air, so I opened my eyes and saw David climbing inside with me. I thought he was sound asleep on the couch. The cold draft made my nipples hard.

"Excuse me, sir," I said to David as he touched my back.

"Relax, it's just a shower," David said as he reached for the soap.

The bar of soap fell to the bottom of the tub and we

couldn't help but laugh. That laugh broke the weird-ass vibe. "Woah!" I said, noticing that his dick was already rock hard. I kept my cool.

We locked eyes and it was on. He grabbed my sponge and scrubbed my back. Then he quickly dropped the sponge and used his tongue to lick my back down to my ass. He slapped my ass one good time. It stung like hell but felt good at the same time. He grabbed my hair and pushed me onto the glass, rubbing his dick against my ass. I started leaking down my leg. I couldn't tell if it was water or the juices from my pussy. He slid the tip of his dick inside me from behind, and I moaned loudly.

"You are mine for life," he said. He began to long-stroke me, and after a few minutes, I screamed as cum sprang from my pussy. The first time we had sex, he'd cum quick, but now I was the one who couldn't hold back. Maybe it was the words, maybe it was the liquor. He screamed too, so I guess we were bussing at the same time. After he pulled out, I slid down the shower wall and onto the floor.

He pulled me up. "Let's get in the bed," he said.

We lay in bed, both looking up at the ceiling. I smiled and he looked at me.

"You all right?" he asked.

"Yes."

He rolled over on top of me and kissed my lips then my nipples, down to my pussy. He left his hands on my breasts, caressing them. We had never done it like this before, never in the shower or so spontaneously, and definitely never back to back. I lay there and and watched his head turn left and right, his wet tongue going crazy. Once he felt me cum in his mouth, he kissed his way back up. I thought he was about to kiss me, but he flipped me over and entered me from the back. Now why would he dick me down like this, knowing he was leaving for college in a few weeks? At this point, I didn't want him to go away. I enjoyed the in-house dick almost every night.

"Give me five minutes, and we'll be back at it again," he promised.

"Shiiiiiit," I mumbled.

I waited for him to laugh, but that muthafucka fell asleep and was snoring. I figured he was worn out. It wasn't too long before I followed. I had to be up early for the salon. It was grand re-opening day tomorrow.

CHAPTER 3

ALTHOUGH I HAD just gone to sleep, I was excited to get up and reveal the newly remodeled shop to all my friends and my mother's friends. I couldn't stop thinking about how proud my mother would be to see her vision of her salon/boutique come to light. She had this space for over five years, but all her money kept going into repairs and inventory. She would be proud that her teenage daughter took the money she left and upgraded the design of the salon. It was a new, modern look; everything she ever talked about from the floor plans to the paint—I made sure it was done right. I remembered every conversation we had about her plans. After she had a long day, she would always come home and flop on the couch with her wine and say that one day her salon would be the talk of the town.

"Today is that day, Mama," I said, looking up at the ceiling, assuming Heaven was real and she could hear me.

I pranced around the house, playing music and twirling, putting together the cutest outfit.

"All that dancing is from this dick last night?" David said while holding his boxer shorts and scaring me because I didn't hear him walk in the dining room.

"Of course it is," I said, playing along with him.

"Do you want me to whip up breakfast?"

"I'm good. I'm actually about to jump in the shower so I can run out of here."

"You want me to join you?" David joked.

"Nooooo!" I sang.

"Who all did you invite to the grand opening?"

"The usual," I said.

"That means just me and Britt."

"Wow, David."

"Wow, what? You are a loner, Jaz!"

"That's right, but this is business, so just get ready to see."

"Well, excuse me, Miss Business Woman. Just know I am proud of you."

"Thanks, bae. I really got to get out of here."

It took me all of thirty minutes to get clean and out the door.

"Bae, make sure you lock the door behind you when

you leave. I'm going to get a head start," I said to David as I rushed out the door. I was anxious to get there.

When I arrived at the shop, there were already a few people standing around, waiting on the reveal. Most of them were older clients of my mom's. I greeted a few as I walked past, then went inside and locked the door behind me. I was amazed with the new look and the personalized setup by Haute Kutuer Events. I gave them my idea and they made my new salon perfect. I stood in the middle of the floor and looked around by myself. I admired all the changes and the money I'd invested. My mom had left me a nice amount of money from her insurance policy, and I was sure to put it back into the place she created.

Every workstation had a different picture of my mom mounted above the mirror. The lights were bright, and the boutique side was full of new clothing items. Everything was perfect; the only thing missing was my mom.

David arrived after an hour, and I was ready to open the door to the community my mom loved. The neighborhood needed to see the new boss in town.

"Are you ready, Jaz? The line outside is crazy, and the nosy people are ready to judge and talk," David said, holding my hand.

I nodded and unlocked the door to let everyone in.

"Wow, Jaz, this is nice!" my mom's salon sisters said as they walked in. They were the first to see the place since it was their new work home. They hadn't been in this place in two months and were excited to get their spaces back.

Cultivating Catering by Chrissy provided the food. The presentation was nice. The hood muthafuckas ran straight in and directly to the food. A few others ran right over to the Tipsy Tea display to get samples of the strawberry lemonade Henny. Half the people were there to be nosy. I heard a lady whisper, "She did well with that lil' insurance money." I couldn't even entertain the negativity because I noticed Miss B walking up with a wrapped gift and a huge smile.

"Attention, everyone," Miss B said on the microphone.

"What's this?" I questioned after she passed me the gift.

"Open it."

I opened the neatly wrapped purple box and couldn't believe my eyes. It was a salon apron that had a picture of my mom on the front and the words *You Got This, Jaz* on the top.

My eyes filled with water as I stared at the beautiful picture of my mother.

"Jaz, we are proud of you for rebuilding a better salon home for us. You are young and smart, and we are happy to be a part of your new journey." Miss B had the spotlight on me as I blushed.

"Thank you, Miss B."

"That's my bitch! Ayee!" Britt screamed from across the room.

"OMG," I said under my breath.

Britt was drunk. I could hear it in her voice from far away. I know Britt, and she was about to make this moment about herself.

"Jaz, be sure to network with the people in here so you can get some customers for your boutique and some new clients. Don't rush over there to your little ghetto friend," Miss B said as she grabbed the gift from me so my hands could be free. I waved to get David's attention.

"David, please go over and keep Britt company so she can be calm. You know how she acts when she's not getting any attention."

"Sure, baby, anything you need."

Miss B, who was one of my mom's best friends and business partners, had some heavy hitters at this grand opening. Miss B was the boss in these streets. She was fifty-three years old but she looked as if she were still in her early thirties. She was as light as they come, with jet-black hair that she dyed that way, and she always had it in a ponytail with hair added. She had some pretty white teeth with the cutest small gap. When she smiled, she had the deepest dimples. Miss B loved bragging about how all the guys loved her smile. She grew up in an era where a lot of her friends did drugs, but she said her motto was to date the drug dealer and not do the drugs. That's why she's still one of the OGs in the city with all the connections.

Miss B called in to her plug with the radio station; she had her girl, Frank Robinson from WGCI, set up a station and go live from the store, offering gifts and doing raffles. She also did a live premiere of a new song from Chicago's hottest female rapper, Chella H. Miss B said she wanted to promote the boutique to be one of the hottest stores in Chicago, and that's what she did.

The music was spinning, the crowd was shopping, and the ones who came to spectate did just that. The evening was going great until David took his eye off Britt and she came running over to me.

"Damn, you too busy to hang with me?" Britt said with tension in her voice.

"My bad, G. I've been working the register and mingling with the customers." I tried to smooth things over, hoping she would understand.

"You already letting this lil' shop get to your head," she whispered before walking off.

"You all right?" David walked over and asked.

"Yeah, I'm good. But she is testing my patience. David, please keep her entertained."

"I got you, boo. You looking good," David said, flirting with me.

I felt warm inside from David's comfort and happy from the outcome of this grand opening.

I heard a voice behind me. "Wow! You did your thing, baby girl." When I turned around, I saw chubby-ass Chris holding flowers. My head dropped to my hand, knowing that this night was about to do a 360 once David looked this way.

CHAPTER 4

"WHAT ARE YOU doing here, Chris?"

"You not happy to see me?" Chris questioned me back.

Chris stood there, five foot four and probably 250 pounds. He had hella swag. He was dressed in jeans with a fitted tee that had his belly sticking out even more, and he had the thickest gold chain on that was full of diamonds.

I met Chris about two weeks ago. I was out riding with Britt, having some girl time, bending some blocks, and getting high. As we got into the car, Britt turned the music up and lit her skimpy-ass blunt. She told me which way to go because that was her thing—riding and smoking. My thing was always staying at the crib. I loved being at home. That night, we ended up outside of White Castle, where everybody hung out—car clubs, bike clubs, drug dealers, and, of course, girls our age who were always looking for older guys.

White Castle was *the* spot. There was always somebody out there playing music loud enough for girls to dance to and, of course, as soon as Britt opened the door, she started popping her lil' booty. She always had on the tightest leggings with no panties to give the illusion of an ass, but as soon as her clothes came off, I was sure she had nothing. My girl had a pretty face, though. And Britt had little legs and a little butt but some big-ass titties. My mom would always say, "Your friend needs to invest in a good bra."

As Britt danced, those big-ass titties bounced, damn near coming out of her shirt. She was showing her ass, acting a fool, twerking and being loud as usual. She was always looking for attention, but I loved my G.

I had noticed two guys walking toward us. One was tall and dark just like I liked them, and the other was short and chubby but had on a lot of jewelry, all flashy just like Britt liked her guys. She swore she was about to get saved by a nigga. Britt was just twerking away; I didn't think she even noticed them coming, but knowing her ass and how hard she was twerking, she probably did.

The chubby, flashy dude was staring at me, and I shook my head. *Please, look the other way,* I thought. But just as I suspected, as soon as they walked up, he approached me.

"I'm Chris. What's your name, beautiful?"

"Jaz," I replied but not in the sweetest voice.

He followed up with the lamest questions ever. "Do you have a man? Can I get to know you?"

I was sure he didn't give a fuck if I had a man. "Nope,

I don't have a man, and getting to know me is not a good idea. I'm going through so much shit right now that getting to know me ain't even worth it."

I noticed Britt was smiling and smoking with the dark-skinned cutie. Chris didn't care about my attitude because he kept talking. "Whatever you going through, sweetheart, I don't need to know. I just want to be a part of your life to make you smile."

I finally smiled back at him. That was some smooth-ass shit. I could see why the young chicks always talked to the older guys.

His face lit up. "There it goes, that pretty smile, those pretty teeth. I want to put a thousand smiles on your face if you let me."

He had me smiling, and that's how he got my number. We had been talking and texting ever since that night. I never had time to link up with him because of everything I had going on with the shop and being under David. Some nights, our phone conversations got deep, and we had promised to meet, but plans always fell through. I didn't expect him to show up here because I didn't invite him. There was only one person who could have invited him, and when I looked up, she was staring right at us.

Britt's sneaky ass was smiling and talking to his friend. I had told Britt that Chris and I had been chopping it up on the phone. She asked me several times if she could invite him just so his friend could come, and I told her no.

Chris was standing to my left, holding red roses. It

wasn't long before I noticed David's facial expression that read, "What the fuck?" He started walking toward me with his lips poked out and his eyes radiating anger. David was always protective of me, even before we started having sex. I know the sex got him superglued to me now. Chris handed me the flowers and reached for a second hug. I couldn't be an asshole, so, of course, I hugged him back.

"Who is your friend, Jaz?" David asked right away.

"David, this is Chris, and Chris, this is David."

We were interrupted by Britt's stupid, high ass. "Yeah, this is David, our *friend*. Nothing major, right?" she said sarcastically.

David and I looked at Britt at the same time, noticing how drunk and high she was. I couldn't believe she showed up to my event like this. What I couldn't understand the most was why she would invite Chris, especially after I told her no repeatedly.

David still had a mean mug when he walked off. It was awkward as hell standing next to Chris while he looked at me as if he wanted to eat me. It wasn't long before Britt grabbed the attention again; she had the nerve to pull a blunt out her purse and attempt to light it right in front of all my mom's friends.

In a low voice, I said, "Britt, hold that down until we leave."

Britt gave me the dirtiest look as if I did something to her. She was lucky I wasn't dragging her across this floor for being rude and inviting Chris.

"Bitch, please," Britt stated dramatically. "Don't stand here and act like you don't smoke. Stop acting all cute in your lil' shop."

"Britt, calm the fuck down or get out!" I spat back.

Miss B approached. "Is everything OK, Jaz?"

"Yes, old lady," Britt screamed.

Before Miss B could snatch her up, David rushed to grab Britt. He instructed Chris and his friend to leave with her. I thanked Chris for the roses as he walked behind Britt, but he didn't look back at me. I think he was a little embarrassed by Britt's actions as well.

I was livid with Britt. I tried to hold myself together, but she walked back in screaming, "Where is my purse?" As soon as she got close enough to me, I attempted to grab her, but David caught my hand and Miss B ran over in the middle of us. "You think you so much better than me that you want to fight me now, Jaz? I'll give you your moment, extra-ass bitch, you been acting different since you came across that lil' money your mom left for you," Britt spat at me.

"What? You think I give a fuck about some money when I'm missing my mom? You sound real jealous, but that's nothing new coming from you, Britt. I tried to put your actions today on the liquor, but this is your true self showing."

"Jealous? Of someone who is drinking alcohol for breakfast and popping pills for lunch? Yeah, Miss Perfect, did David know that? Miss B, while you holding me back, did y'all know that Little Miss Perfect was smoking, drinking, and popping pills every night?"

I couldn't take another word. I reached around Miss B and grabbed Britt by her nappy-ass weave. David grabbed my hand, detaching it from her hair, and as soon as she could, she ran out the door. I was heated.

"How dare that bum bitch come to my event and act an ass?"

"Well, money makes people change, baby," Miss B said while picking up a few things that fell over.

"Just relax. Let's lock up and head to your crib," David said, still holding my arm until we saw Britt get into somebody's car and pull off.

"I will clean and lock up everything, David, just get her home," Miss B said.

I was heated during the entire drive home. I couldn't believe the nerve of that nosy-ass bitch to blow up my spot. But hey, my mama never liked her and always told me to watch out for fake-ass friends.

After leaving the shop, David and I pulled up at the same time. Good thing we drove separately because I needed every bit of the drink I left in my car. Although, I was surprised we arrived at the same time because I needed an extra ten minutes to get upstairs to pop my last Perc without him on my back.

David stopped to grab tacos. He always had good food for our Netflix-and-chill nights. I planned to play sleep if he asked me any questions about Chris or about anything that

Britt said. David knew I was drinking heavy, but he had no idea that I was smoking so much weed and popping pills. I decided to leave the roses Chris got me inside the car. I didn't want to spark the conversation, but knowing David, he would bring it up. I couldn't blame him.

When we got upstairs, we both dove into the food. This was one long-ass day. I was messed up thinking about my argument with Britt and how she attempted to ruin my event. I kept my cool by looking down and eating my food. I kept stuffing my mouth just in case David wanted to bring up some of the things she said or—better yet—bring up Chris.

"These tacos are fire. I'm going to miss this good-ass food while I'm at school," David said with a full mouth as we sat at the table, enjoying what we did most nights: eat good food then have good sex.

As soon as we locked eyes, and he was sipping his ice cold lemonade, I felt it coming. That statement about the damn tacos was only how he got me to look up.

"So, what's that shit Britt was talking about when y'all were arguing? Are you really popping pills, Jaz?" he asked.

"I really don't want to talk about it. She's a hating-ass bitch and that's just that."

"Jaz, we can find you help if you can't stop the drinking and whatever else you're doing. You are too smart and pretty, and we both know your mom wouldn't want this for you."

"Please don't say shit about my mom. We don't know what she wants. She's dead! I'm here alone, by myself, so don't mention her name ever again," I shouted.

I could tell by his uneasy face he wanted to keep going about the pills, but tears started falling from my eyes. I was in extra-dramatic mode. David could never take my tears, so just like the sweetheart he was, he grabbed me to lead me to the couch. He held me as we watched one of our favorite shows. The night faded away in silence.

We were woken up around six in the morning by multiple texts from Britt. She texted us both in a group text: *I know y'all probably together like y'all have been the last few weeks and I am very hurt that it's been more of y'all two instead of all three of us. I don't want to make excuses but that's where my attuide came from last night. I do apologize for showing up to your event, ruining your special moment, and bringing uninvited guests.*

David tried to respond but I snatched his phone. "Fuck that bitch," I said, tossing his phone on the other end of the couch.

"She apologized to you, Jaz. Can you forgive her?"

"Not now. She's a hater."

"Was she telling the truth about the pills, Jaz?"

"Here you go," I mumbled.

"If I didn't care, I wouldn't ask. And I don't want to go away and be worried that you are trying to kill yourself popping that poison."

"That's exactly why I have to hide what I'm doing as if I'm a child. Because you are quick to judge."

"Wow! That's what you think of me?" David said as he

slipped his black Air Force 1s on and started walking to the door.

"Yeah, that's what I think. Go ahead and leave. I have had better people leave out my door and never return."

The door slammed and I went straight to my phone to reply to our group text. I was heated at this moment.

Both you bitches can stay away from me for life!

CHAPTER 5

TEARS FELL FROM my eyes as I fought the urge to pop this last pill. I had been trying to stop on my own, but I knew deep inside I needed help. I'd been numbing myself for too long. I reached for my phone to check for any more texts from David. I knew he would check on me even though I pissed him off. He never went more than an hour without texting me, and now it had been almost eight hours since he stormed out the door.

I hadn't moved from the couch. I laid there, going through my phone, looking at pictures and old videos of my mom, and feeling empty inside. I was going through a lot for my age—juggling a new business and a bank account full of money—and the only thing that made me truly happy was getting high.

Ding ding. My phone finally went off, and it was a text from David as I expected: *Are you calm now?*

Even though I had waited on the text, I didn't reply. Instead, I decided to text Chris, thanking him for the flowers but also trying to ease my way in a conversation to see if Britt got the Percs from him. If I did take my last pill, I would need a new supplier because Britt and I were never talking again. She had shown her hater hand, and I couldn't forgive that.

My mom was set up and killed by a hating-ass friend, and I refused to have people around me that I couldn't trust. Britt knew that more than anybody. That's why I couldn't accept her apology.

Chris texted back immediately. *What's up, shorty? I didn't expect a text from you.*

Why is it a shocker that I text thank you? I'm not an asshole, I replied.

Is your security boyfriend sitting next to you monitoring these texts? Lol.

First off, that's not my boyfriend. And second, if he was anything special I wouldn't have texted you in the first place.

OK, I hear you, shorty.

Jaz or Jazzy. You can call me any of those, just not shorty. OK, shorty?

Well, damn!

I replied, *LOL,* but I wasn't smiling. I really hated being called "Shorty" by anyone. Everyone needed to recognize I was a grown-ass woman.

Wyd? You want to step out? Chris asked.

Nah, I'm cool. I was just shooting you a thank you.

Aight. But if you really want to thank me, let me take you out.

I'll think about it. I smiled while texting this because I had never been asked out on a date before. David and I had been friends so long, we never went out on dates. We just got food and stayed at the crib.

After coming out of my text thread with Chris, I noticed that David had texted four times. Three of the texts were just my name and the fourth text was him saying he was on his way. He probably assumed I was ignoring him. I didn't want to be bothered with him; I was still gloating about being asked on a real date.

My phone rang, and I could see that it was the doorman's desk.

"Hi, Jaz. You have a guest by the name of David here in the lobby. Should I send him up?"

Umm no, I thought.

But I said, "Sure, send him up. And thanks for calling."

I jumped off the couch, looking just the way I did when he left, and stood by the door, waiting on him to come in with his sorry-ass vibe.

As soon as David hit the door, he said, "Jaz, I'm sorry for walking out like that."

"It's cool," I said while trying to see what he had behind his back.

"I got you an Italian beef dipped with cheese and extra hot peppers, just the way you like."

"You sure do know how to buy forgiveness," I said, reaching for the bag. We sat and ate at the table. I finally took a deep breath and said I was sorry too for overreacting.

We ate and chilled out, which was our repeated cycle. I was tired of it and I wanted to be outside kicking it. I wanted to shop and feel free. David was a typical teenager; he didn't have extra money to spend, so us going shopping together wasn't possible. We played it safe by staying in all the time, watching TV and eating good, then he would always end the night by eating *me* good. I couldn't stunt. He did give some good spontaneous head any chance he could: in the car, the shower, the back of my shop. He said my walk made him want to eat me alive, and that's just what he did.

We repeated our cycle each and every day throughout the summer. I was still texting Chris a lot. We made plans, but I kept breaking them because David didn't give me a break. He was always at my house or at the shop. It had been three weeks with no pills or alcohol for me, and I guess I could thank David for that because he stayed on my ass. I knew deep inside he wanted the best for me, but did I want the best for myself? I always questioned that.

CHAPTER 6

THE DAY WAS here, and I was ready to be free now. I was ecstatic about David leaving. I would miss the sex, but I was ready to be free of routines.

Chris and I had been texting so much, and I felt bad for always sending him off about meeting up. I did love David, but I was tired of love at the moment. I was ready to have some much-needed fun. The last few weeks, I'd stalked all my high school buddies' Instagram pages and they had been living life. Now that David was leaving, it was only right that I partook in some hood activity.

I went to David's mom's house to see him leave. David was all packed up and ready to go. His mom and sisters were trailing him to college. His school was only a few hours away, and he insisted on taking his own car. He didn't want to be stuck there if anything were to happen in the city with his mom or sisters and, of course, me. His mom offered me an invite to ride with her, but it was Saturday, which was a big day for the boutique, especially with everyone leaving for college and coming to grab a few things for school. I needed to be there to watch the cash.

David didn't want to let me go; he kept holding me, saying he didn't want to leave me. He even kissed me down. "Ew!" his sisters said in unison before their mom pointed at them to get in the car. It was hard for David to let me go, but his mom called his name and just like that, he was off to his new world.

I headed to the boutique, and just as I expected, there were plenty of cars parked out front. Even Britt stopped by before she left. We had agreed to have a sit-down and discuss our issues, and I had a box of things waiting for her. We hadn't been on the same page since the reveal party, but deep inside, that was my girl, and I had promised her that when she left for school, I would give her some of the old inventory of clothes and a few new pieces so she could look good on campus. I kept my promise, and she wasn't turning down free clothes.

Britt was standing outside the shop, waiting on me. As soon as I walked up, she grabbed me and hugged me tight.

"Jaz, I'm so sorry and I miss you so much."

I couldn't respond. I wanted to forgive her and I wanted it to be normal, but something in me just couldn't trust her.

"It's cool," I replied as I hugged her back.

"Jaz, I know you are still hurt about me messing up grand reveal day. I was tripping, G."

"It's cool, Britt. Come grab the bag. I really have to get to work, and I know you should be on the road," I said, rushing her.

Although we agreed on letting it go, Miss B wasn't having it.

I noticed Britt's mama peeping out the window of the car. As soon as we walked in the shop, Miss B stared me down, and I knew I was about to hear a mouthful when Britt left.

Miss B was so much like my mom. She did not like Britt at all, and after the show she put on a few weeks ago, Miss B said she didn't ever want to see Britt near the shop.

Britt and I hugged again, but I could tell we would never be friends again. The energy wasn't there. We were once inseperable, but after repeated times of slick, hating words and fallouts, our vibe wasn't the same.

"Love you, Jazzzzzzz," Britt sang as she walked out the door with her big bag of free clothes.

"Your mama always said you had a soft heart," Miss B said, spinning in her salon chair as she waited for her client to finish drying.

"What are you talking about?"

"That big-ass bag of free clothes you just gave that girl."

"That was nothing but free promo. She will wear it at school and when they ask her where it came from, she will direct them to our new website or Instagram page."

"Oh, well, your mom always said you were a genius too," she said, laughing.

We always tried to have a good vibe in the shop; although I was the youngest stylist, she treated me with respect.

After such a long day at the shop and saying my goodbyes to David, I was ready to get home and soak in a bath. The boutique side of the shop kept me busy and it made me respect my mother's hustle ten times as much. Working hard wasn't a problem for me because I'd be damned if my mother's dream went down the drain. This was her pride and joy. This was what made her happy. She died protecting it.

I had planned a nice day for the next day in my head that included retail therapy. I loved living near the downtown area. I was just a cab or Uber ride away from all the designer stores and good restaurants. It was time to go shopping for some new drip. I had been holding on to my money—other than the amount I'd put into the salon.

As soon as I walked into the Louis Vuitton store, Taylor, the sales associate, ran over to hug me. He was wearing the brightest colors and the biggest smile. He held me tight as if we were first cousins at a family reunion. I wiggled loose to take a deep breath.

"Where is Mom?" Taylor said in his jubilant voice.

It was clear that Taylor hadn't heard about my mother,

and he wouldn't hear about it today because I was in a happy place and wanted to stay there as long as I could.

"Now, Taylor, I hope you got the new combat boots, size thirty-eight?" I said.

"The boot is tall and comfortable. I knew you or your mom would be picking them up. It's your type of style, and it has a cross-body bag to match."

"Oh, yeah, Taylor! You know the rule: no new shoes without a matching bag."

"Of course, honey," we said in unison, wiggling our fingers.

As I sat waiting on Taylor to bring the boots, I scrolled on my phone, just waiting on a post from Britt or David. I really didn't post on social media, but I kept all my accounts to be nosy. I was shocked they hadn't posted anything about their new college life.

"Jaz, Jaz!"

I was staring at my phone when I heard somebody calling my name. I kept my attention on the phone, hoping whoever it was would think it wasn't me and keep moving. Within seconds, I felt somebody tapping on my shoulder. *Who the fuck?* I thought, and when I looked up, it was Chris.

I smiled as I looked up at his cute, chubby face. He had the 360–degree waves spinning in his head as if he just took off his durag.

"What's up, stranger?" I asked.

He hit me right back with that smooth-ass shit he was

spitting the night I met him. "I don't have to be a stranger," he said.

I laughed but tried to keep cool. "What you doing in my favorite store?"

"I'm just down here copping some shit, and as I walked past the window, I peeped a fat ass hanging off this seat, so I had to come see who it was. And it was just who I needed it to be."

"So you just be hollering at any ol' body with a fat ass, huh?"

Chris made a face, but he kept the conversation going. "What you in here getting?" he asked.

Before I could tell him, Taylor walked over and gave me the boots. "Hello, Chris," Taylor said.

"What up, Tay?" Chris replied.

Chris must've been a regular as well. I felt uncomfortable trying the boots on in front of Chris, so I told Taylor to take them to the register.

"Damn, baller. You just throwing it in the bag, huh?" Chris said.

"Nah, I'm just treating myself," I replied.

"Well, treat me too, boss lady," Chris said, waving a belt at me that he was holding.

"Tuh!"

"You can't treat ya boy to this cheap-ass belt?"

"Damn, you must be a jigalow," I said, laughing.

"I'm just playing with you, shorty, I got my own bag of money."

"Well, spend that shit!" I said as I walked toward the register.

I thought Chris was walking behind me since he was talking that money shit, but when I reached the register and looked back, he was gone like a thief in the night.

CHAPTER

ONCE I FINISHED my transaction and had a few more giggles with Taylor, I headed out the door. As I walked down the street, I heard my name.

"Well, if it isn't Houdini himself," I said as he ran up to me.

"Girl, what you talking about?" Chris said, breathing heavy.

I smiled and watched him catch his breath.

I should've kept walking because I just knew his chubby ass wouldn't have caught up with me. He had a bag from another store, so apparently that was where he'd dipped to.

"Let me carry that big-ass bag for you." Chris reached his hand out.

The big orange bag was heavy, so I handed it to him.

"What you on today? Let's walk across the street and grab some food at Grand Lux."

I was starving, so I said, "Fuck it; let's go. But promise me you won't run out on the bill."

"Don't play me like I'm not the man."

As we entered the restaurant, Chris was greeted by the host with all smiles. "Hey, Chris! You want your usual spot? It's open today."

"Yeah, that's cool."

"I see you, playa. You must bring all yo' hoes here," I said.

"Stop it," he said as he pulled my chair back so I could sit down.

"A gentleman, you are," I said, smiling.

This seat had the perfect view of downtown Michigan Ave. I could see all the stores and the tall buildings. I guess this was my first date. With my life moving so fast, I never had time to be on an actual date. I thought it would be like the movies: me getting all dressed up with a dress and heels. This was a hood edition: we sat at the table surrounded by a Louis Vuitton bag and Nike bags.

"Damn, your lips are pretty," Chris said, staring at my face.

I licked my lips, saying, "Thank you."

"Girl, don't turn me on at this table, licking your lips."

"My bad." I giggled.

Once the food came, he ate his wings and fries fast. I sat there trying to eat pretty, knowing damn well I wanted to throw that whole wing down my throat and slide the bone back out my mouth.

"Yo' shop and boutique is really popping on the streets," Chris said.

"Thank you, I'm trying."

"Nah, for real! You are doing your thing. You are young, pretty, and bossed up."

"Thanks for noticing."

"*Shit,* who don't notice? I feel honored to be out with you right now."

Smacking my lips and smiling from ear to ear, I said, "Stop it." Chris was stroking my ego with all this sweet talk.

"Do you want kids?" he asked out of the blue.

"Hell no!"

"Damn, why you say it like that? Usually females want babies."

"Not me. I'm the baby. Better yet, my salon is the baby. I'm building something right now."

"Damn, you are so mature. Usually pretty bitches be bird brains."

"What?"

"No offense to you." He hurried to try to clear it up.

"You look like you got a lot of kids," I said.

"Damn, I do?"

"Yep!"

"What do a guy with kids look like?"

"You! Fine and charming. I'm sure you slipped in a lot of panties."

"Wow, you really judging me. Do you want to know what you look like?"

"I'm scared to know."

"You look like my future wife."

I smiled, speechless, as he charmed me again. When the bill came, I reached for my wallet, but he tried to stunt and laid two stacks on the table.

"Put them little peanuts away, shorty," he said.

I wanted to talk my shit, but he kept stunting, so I just listened.

"I could have bought that lil' shit at LV for you, but you ran to the register so fast—"

"Nah, don't play with me. You know your ass disappeared," I snapped.

"Stop it, G. I'm a real-ass nigga."

"We'll see."

"You damn right because I'm going to have to show you."

These Chicago guys always talked about what they could've done, but we knew those who wanted to do it really just did it. I couldn't keep listening to him stunt; I had to let him know about me because he obviously had me confused.

I looked him in his eyes and said, "Look, I'm not one of these little girls out here that needs you for your money. Anything I want, I can buy it twice on some real young boss-ass shit."

"Damn, shorty, I fuck with you, but your money don't mean shit if you not having fun with it. I got to get you out here to start having fun. It's real shit to do in these streets, and you don't have to stay cooped up in your apartment every day."

I coughed a little. "Condo."

"Well, damn, excuse me, Miss Boss Bitch!"

"Are you a stalker?" I asked. "How do you know what I do?"

"Well, I never see you outside. I used to see Britt outside a lot, and every time I asked about you, she said you stay in the house."

"So, you have been looking for me?"

"Hell yeah!" he said with the biggest smile.

I got up and walked away from the table once the waitress gave Chris his change. I poked my ass out as I walked in front of him, headed toward the door. It was still sunny outside, and it felt a little too good to go in the house.

Chris had to be thinking the same thing because we barely hit the door before he spat out, "You want to go bowling? I finally got you outside now." He had the biggest Kool-Aid smile I'd ever seen. There was a bowling alley a mile away we could walk to. As we walked and talked, he seemed interesting, but he never said what he did for a living. I assumed he did some scam shit because when he put his money on the table at the restaurant, I saw a few debit cards fall out of his pocket, and one of them was a Hello Kitty Bank of America debit card, so I knew he'd probably gotten a fresh college student out of her shit.

I was really feeling Chris, maybe because he was older or maybe because he talked slick.

With all that walking and talking, we arrived at Lucky Strike quickly. I'd never been there before. It was nice, with good lighting, a bar, and other games to play. I'd never bowled before. Every time I went to a bowling alley in high school, it was always just to link up and talk shit with my friends. I didn't tell Chris I couldn't bowl; I let him see it for himself.

Bowling went exactly how I thought it would go—he busted my ass. He won three games back to back to back. He showed me how to hold the ball and how to center it. I got the position right, but I kept acting like I forgot so he could get behind me and put his dick on my ass. But shit, it might've just been his stomach I was feeling.

Chris was dressed comfortably like me. He wore gray joggers with some fresh whites and a hoodie. I had on my gray stacked leggings with a gray crop hoodie and fresh Adidas white shell toes before I changed into the raggedy red and gray bowling shoes. Those shoes did not match my swag, but it was either be cute or slip and bust my shit with regular shoes on this shining bowling floor. I was being a perv, trying to get a glimpse of his dick print through his joggers. He had a nice bulge peeking through his pants. I know he caught me looking because he smiled at me once we locked eyes again.

When I finally pulled my phone out of my purse, I saw that I had over ten missed calls from David. Chris must have seen my face because he said, "Damn, what's wrong? Your man been hitting you up?"

I ignored his question as I skimmed through all of David's texts asking me if I was all right. After placing my phone back in my purse, I gathered my things to leave. We had been at the bowling alley for over two hours.

"Where is your dope-ass whip?" I asked him as we were walking out the door. "With all the shit you talk, I know you got to be riding nice," I added before he could answer my question.

"I parked over by The Water Tower, and you talk as much shit as I do, so where is yours?"

"My car is at home. I don't live too far from here. I'm actually about to jump in a cab, so I'll holler later." I was surprised he didn't question me about where I stayed; instead, he reached for a hug.

"Can I get a kiss?" He laughed because he must've known I was going to say hell no.

"Give me your cheek," I said.

He leaned in, but as soon as I went for his cheek, he turned his head, and our lips met. *Son of a bitch*, I thought as I wiped my lips and walked off.

He laughed again. "Sorry, I had to. Them lips are perfect, and I can only imagine how them lips in your pants look." He had a cool look on his face as nasty words came out of his mouth.

The taxi was pulling up, so I ran, but I looked back and smiled at his crazy ass.

During my ten-minute ride home, I couldn't stop thinking about whether I was wrong or not for my little outing with Chris. I couldn't take my thoughts off that kiss, either. David and I weren't official, but in an odd way it felt like I was out cheating on him. If he asked where I had been, should I tell him? Before I knew it, I was pulling up at home. I paid the cab driver and texted David at the same time. This was the third text I sent him since I'd noticed all those missed calls. He could've been ignoring me, but I was too tired to figure it out. I figured I'd give him his space. I'd had long day.

Once I got upstairs, I didn't even try on my new boots. I went straight for the shower then lay across my bed, naked. I started thinking about Chris, so I texted him, telling him I was home. He didn't respond, either. He was probably out wining and dining the next bitch. Guys like Chris seemed to have a lot of action.

I called David. Still no answer, but I couldn't get mad because of all the calls I'd missed from him. Before I knew it, I was out like a light.

My phone notification went off, and when I looked at the clock on my nightstand, I saw that it was 5:46 a.m. I looked at the phone and saw Monica's number. I didn't pick up the first time she called because I figured if it was something important, Britt would've called no matter how mad she was. The third time she called, I picked up, and it wasn't nice. "Monica, what do you want this damn early?" I asked, annoyed.

"Bitch, why you ain't tell me Britt and David was a couple?"

"What are you talking about, Monica? It's too early for fake drama."

"Ain't nothing fake, Jaz, look at your phone. I just sent a picture of them in the same damn bed, naked! I should've known something was up because the upperclassmen threw a welcome party for the freshmen yesterday, and those two were up under each other the entire time, taking shots and giggling."

What the fuck? I looked at my messages, and I couldn't believe my eyes. My heart shattered like a chandelier falling from the ceiling. David and Britt were naked, and he was holding her the same way he held me night after night. I was livid!

CHAPTER 8

THREE HOURS AFTER tossing and turning from that news Monica just gave me, my alarm went off. I muted it but my mind was racing with thoughts. I quickly jumped out the bed and grabbed my purse from the chair in the corner of my room. I went rumbling through it, looking for a piece of pill, an old piece of blunt … anything to stop my mind from going full speed. I was sick to my stomach just thinking of the pic Monica sent me. That messy bitch knew what she was doing too. After searching my purse high and low, I couldn't find anything to take my mind off this bullshit. Several questions went through my mind. How could David do this? Did I deserve this since I went on a date with Chris? What was Britt thinking?

"Fuck!" I screamed out loud. *A blunt would really ease my mind right now. Chris should know where I can get some pills from.* I was hesitant to text him so early this morning. "Think, Jaz, think," I mumbled to myself as I paced the kitchen floor. I was so mad!

I was more upset with David and all the false hope he sold me about getting his degree and being my future husband. We could throw that idea straight out the window because I would never marry any man that Britt fucked.

I finally noticed a full bottle of Hennessy that I forgot all about since I had slowed down drinking. It wasn't noon yet, and I cracked the bottle open so fast, I didn't even have a cup. I took it straight to the head. I wanted to be numb. Numb to memories, numb to pain. I sat on my couch, still naked, still ignoring the alarms on my phone. I had a client today, but I refused to leave this house.

My stomach started to burn after so many head-up shots, and I started to get really hot and dizzy. I attempted to run to the bathroom but tripped over my big-ass orange Louis bag that was still sitting in the middle of the floor. *Oh shit,* I thought. Vomit came flying out my mouth and onto my plush white carpet. After vomiting, my stomach felt better but my head was spinning. I could barely move. I was lying right next to the yellow vomit on the floor, just staring at the ceiling. My phone was ringing, but it was too far for me to reach. So I laid there, balled up, holding my stomach and praying that the room would stop spinning.

Suddenly there was a repeated knock on the door. "Ugh," I said out loud as my elbow touched the vomit once I rolled over.

"Jaz, are you in there?" I heard a male voice from the other side of the door.

"Yes, who is it?" I shouted back, still trying to pull my aching body from the floor.

"It's Carlos, the building maintenance man. We had a call from someone named Miss B to do a well-being check. She asked if you can please call her regarding the shop."

"Thank you," I shouted back as I was finally able to pull myself from the floor. I got my phone from the couch. Woah. It was almost 8:00 p.m. I could barely remember how I got on the floor. When I looked at my phone again, I saw that it was on two percent battery life and I had thirty-four missed calls. Most were from Miss B and the others were from David. What the fuck could he possibly want?

I went to my text messages. I got a glimpse of a text from Chris, but before I could read it, I was interrupted by a call coming in from Miss B.

"Damn! What the fuck, Jaz?" Miss B yelled through the phone.

"My bad," I said in a low voice.

"Jaz, I don't know what you on, but you had a client here waiting on you, and that's not cool. You supposed to be 'bout this business, but today, you proved that you're not ready." Miss B hung that phone up dead in my face, and I was glad she did because I didn't have a lie or an excuse ready. I felt horrible about standing my client up and passing out on the floor. This shit made me ten times madder at David and Britt. I walked over to the couch where I left the bottle of Hennessy, picked it up, and flung the bottle across the room. I went back to my room to try to rest in my bed, praying my headache went away.

I jumped up like it was the first day of school and I was thirsty to wear a new outfit. After tossing and turning all night, I had pulled myself together because no matter what was going on, I had shit to do, and I had to prove I was ready for this new boss world. Of course, I wanted to reach out to those bitches, but what good would that do me if they were away and I was here? I had a lot of time to think last night as I slept off and on. This shit was far from over, and I planned on getting down to the bottom of it. David could have slept with anybody else in the world—even Monica, his old love—but our bestie? That's the part that didn't sit right with me.

I was showered and set to leave. Luckily my client from yesterday wasn't too mad and agreed to come back today.

I arrived at the shop right on time. My client was arriving at the same time. I had a closed-off section in the back because I wasn't licensed yet. Every dollar I made from doing hair would be saved up so I could eventually expand the salon even bigger. I also wanted to add some barbers to the mix of things. I was lucky to have experience doing hair in my mom's basement long before all of this happened. My mom knew I had the talent, but she never wanted me to be addicted to the fast money.

My client was in and out. I was ready to do this forever. Hell, forty dollars an hour—I couldn't beat that! Once I got a license, I'd raise my prices like every other beautician in our city—sixty dollars and up. But I would always wash and blow dry with every style, unlike eighty percent of the stylists in my city. My mom called that the *new age thing*.

I sat in the shop for hours. I was on the boutique side for a while, training the intern. I knew having a high school student work the boutique would be an advantage because all her classmates would come shop. My mom used me the same way, and I had my entire school buying up all the clothes, especially at tax time, using their parents' money.

David was blowing up my phone, calling and texting me. I didn't even think about picking up the phone. I wasn't ready for his side of the story. But I did read his text: *What did Monica tell you?*

I wanted to forward the picture Monica sent, but I knew Britt would kill her if she knew she'd snuck a picture.

"Who is this guy with roses walking up?" Miss B said with a smile. I guess she thought it was for her.

I looked from behind my private wall and saw that it was Chris. The way he walked was very distinctive. He walked with a limp and I wanted to ask so bad if he had been shot before; I just assumed it with him being a typical hood guy. Knowing me and my mouth, I was sure I'd get around to asking, but for now I was just being very observant.

"Damn, shorty, you get this fly to come to work? I see you couldn't wait to wear those new boots," he said.

"Don't play with me," I said, reaching for the flowers.

"Excuse me, how do you know these are yours?" he said. "Nah, bae, they're yours, and I came to take you out. Are you done working for today? I tried calling you a few times yesterday. Shit, I thought you were done with me already and we ain't had the real fun yet."

"Nah, it was nothing like that. My bad. Yes, I only had one client. I'm ready to roll out."

I followed Chris to the bowling alley. This time, we both parked in the garage, but I could tell there was going to be a wait because the parking garage was full. I wanted to bowl, but I didn't want to sit around waiting.

When we tried to check in, we found out there was a two-hour wait for lanes, so I told Chris to slide over to my house to watch movies.

"You want to grab a bottle?" Chris asked.

"Hell nah," I replied, damn near grabbing my mouth. I still felt the straight Hennessy from yesterday.

I really tried to stop drinking, but that damn Britt-and-David situation had me back in the bottle. I just needed something to take off the edge of my anger the day before.

"Can I blow this weed in your spot?" Chris was waving a pack of woods at me.

"Hell yeah," I said with excitement. I needed to smoke some loud more than anything right now. Drinking was one thing, but weed was a true healer and I needed to feel that type of peace.

When we arrived back to my spot, he was shocked to see how laid out it was. I basically took all the furniture from my house and hooked my small place up. My living room had a big plush purple sofa and love seat. I had artwork from my favorite movies on the wall. When I wasn't drinking, I was always cleaning and redecorating; that was another way to ease my mind. Before I left for work that morning, I had scrubbed my carpet and put the love seat over the stain so I wouldn't accidentally step in it. I had candles burning all day while I was gone to try to get the liquor and vomit smell out of my place.

"Damn, this is nice," Chris said, plopping on my couch. "Why you don't drink?" he asked.

"I do drink; I'm just on a little break now."

"You can't handle your liquor, lil' mama?"

"Shut up. Yes I can."

"Well, can you handle this?" Chris said, grabbing his dick, which was poking out of the same gray sweat pants he had on the other day.

"Woah there," I said, trying not to stare at how huge his dick was. He started rolling up the weed as if his rock-hard dick was a normal thing. I stood far back from him, contemplating if I was going to do that muthafucka or not.

I turned on a comedy special on Netflix since we were smoking. I was ready to laugh, but of course, we never made it through the beginning of the special before he started kissing my neck, then he lifted my shirt and started kissing on my belly. He pulled my black leggings off, and my lace black thong came down with the pants. He went straight to it, licking my pussy as if it was the first meal he had today. His tongue was going in all the right places.

"Ahhh, Chris!" I screamed, and that made him go crazier with his tongue.

Chris was more experienced than David. He had my whole couch wet. He had his fingers in my ass and his tongue right where it needed to be, and after he ate me, he pulled out his dick. And, goddamn, that muthafuckin' dick was huge! He picked me up and sat me on top of him. My pussy was so wet that his dick went straight in.

"Damn, this pussy is wet and tight," he whispered in my ear as I leaned forward, riding his dick cowgirl style. I was rolling my hips back and forth.

Chris was gigantic, every inch of him touching my walls. I thought David's dick was big, but this grown man's dick hit different.

After what felt like hours, Chris left my knees weak. We fucked three times back to back to back in one night, and his dick never got too soft. He had to be on a pill. I'd heard from other girls I knew that guys on pills never got tired of sex. Most guys in Chicago were either on pills or lean. Whatever it was, there was a big difference between fucking a high school crush and a big, grown-ass man.

Once we finally finished, he didn't go to sleep like David usually did. He got up, hungry.

"You got some food in that state-of-the-art-ass refrigerator?" he asked.

"Sure, help yourself. I'm going to the restroom. I'll be right back."

I went into the bathroom to try to get the sex smell off me. I couldn't take a real shower because I didn't want to leave Chris alone for too long in my house. So I took a towel and washed between my legs and under my breasts. My mom would call it a hoe bath. When I walked out of my bathroom, I noticed Chris standing in the kitchen, eating some leftovers from a week ago. I was going to tell him the food was old, but I looked at the counter and noticed my pile of mail was scattered like someone had been sifting through it. I guessed he was being nosy. That's when I realized it was time for him to go.

"So, yeah, hit me tomorrow," I said, looking at the door.

"Damn, you are putting me out at 2:00 a.m.?"

"I'm not trying to be mean; I'm just tired."

"That's understandable. I know this dick wore you out."

"You got the power; I ain't gon' stunt."

Chris grabbed his things. Once he got to the door, he leaned in for a hug. I couldn't wait for that door to close so I could rush back to my mail to see if anything was open, but my phone rang. It was David again. I didn't pick up. I was ready to block his ass because I didn't care to hear his side of the story—not today.

After Chris left, I thoroughly went through my papers to see if he took anything, but it seemed he'd just looked at every bank statement and bill on the counter. I tossed and turned that entire night because I didn't like people in my business.

A few days passed. Although I had unfinished business with my so-called friends, I had been focusing on myself. I had the same routine every day: going to the shop and checking in on the boutique sales then going to my class. The ladies in the salon pressured me every day about going to get my GED, so I finally enrolled, and it wasn't a bad idea.

Chris tried to come back over to my house a few times, but I turned him down. My walls were sore for a couple of days after he left. I wasn't ready for that again. I thought about the sex often, and it made me horny. We never missed a day of texting or late-night talks. Chris was a cool distraction from David most nights, but I couldn't get David and Britt completely out my head, so I was back drinking.

The GED class was really easy, and the days that I went sober were a breeze. It was more bookwork than I imagined. Some days, I would show up with my coffee cup full of coffee, but on other days I would show up with my coffee cup full of Hennessy and not give a damn about what was being said.

Sundays were my chill day, and I usually looked at different fashion magazines to get a hint of what was hot to make sure my boutique stayed on point. With the Instagram page for the boutique and a few paid promotions from some of the hottest Instagram models, the boutique business was going better than ever. The boutique was my place of peace; I really felt connected to my mother because I was able to create the vision she had.

This Sunday went rather fast. After chilling all day, I was surprised that I didn't receive any calls from Chris. I think my walls were ready for him to enter again. It was odd of him not to send me a text all day. I laid in my bed all night, thinking of the last time we had sex, touching all over myself and wishing he was hitting me from the back. I wanted him next to my body.

The night had gone fast, and I had to be up early for Monday morning because I told a client that booked a photo shoot that I would do her hair before my noon class. As I drove on the I-55, listening to my favorite '90s R&B playlist, I got a call from a strange number with an 866 area code. When I picked up, I heard an automated recording: "This is a collect call from the Cook County Department of Corrections. To accept the charges, press one."

I was curious about who was calling because the recording didn't provide a name. I accepted the charges, and I heard Chris's voice spit out, "Hey, this is Chris. Please don't hang up. Can you please help me out?"

CHAPTER 9

"EXCUSE ME, WHAT are you doing in jail?" I looked at the phone as if he could see me.

He said some bullshit about being in a friend's car and getting pulled over. He said the friend had drugs on him. He also mentioned some debit cards and checks with multiple people's names. I let him finish his story, but I knew whatever they said he did, he did that shit. I had already seen the debit cards at lunch weeks ago.

The phone operator said we had one minute left, and there it was—what I figured the call was really about. "Can you bail me out? It's only fifteen Gs," Chris blurted out.

As soon as he said that, the call was disconnected, and I was relieved. I had only known Chris a few months. Yes, we'd been having fun, and yes, the one time we had sex was bomb, but what the fuck? I was not about to give that nigga fifteen thousand dollars of my savings to get out of jail for some shit I knew he did. My phone rang a few more times with the same number. I needed to think, so I didn't answer it. I heard everything he needed to say in that three-minute call.

My client was coming at 10:00 a.m. and it was already 9:45 a.m. I was thrown off mentally from that call. For some odd reason, I actually considered bailing him out because I wanted to be a down-ass bitch, but I barely knew Chris. I was just thinking of that good dick being locked up.

Whew! Thank God, I was only five minutes late. I got to it, trying to put my confusion in my back pocket. As I spun around in my chair, waiting on my client to dry, a lady walked into the salon, looking around. She looked to be in her forties, but she was dressed very hip. She had on the Louis boots like mine and had a big Louis purse to match, and she wore a black jumpsuit. She looked comfortable but expensive. She reminded me of the way my mom used to dress. She had a brown complexion and wavy hair pulled back with nice edges. She looked like she was from a Caribbean island.

"Hi, can I help you?" I said, walking toward her as she strolled around the shop without saying a thing.

"Hi, I'm looking for Jaz," she said in a hood voice, throwing the Caribbean guess right out the window.

"Who are you?"

"Are you Jaz?"

"Yes, I'm the owner of this shop. Are you trying to make an appointment?"

She smirked. "No."

I could look at her and tell this wavy-headed bitch was about to be a problem.

"Can we talk in private?" she said, walking back toward the door.

"Who the fuck is she?" Miss B said, walking up to me.

"I don't know, B, but she's giving me weird-ass vibes."

"You don't have to be scared, little girl. I'm Chris's mom," the woman said.

"Oh, Chris's mom," I said, still looking puzzled because I didn't know what the fuck she wanted with me. And who the fuck was she calling "little girl"?

"Do you need me to step outside with you?" Miss B asked as she started taking off her coat.

"Nah, I'm good," I said.

I grabbed my little cross-body bag because I kept my small gun in there just in case anybody ever tried to rob me. There had been so many people questioning my money since my mother passed, so I bought a .380. As we stepped outside, Chris's mom looked me up and down.

"I'm Tracy, Chris's mom."

So ... what the fuck you want? I thought. "Hello, and nice to see you. How can I help you?" I asked. I was taught to always show respect.

"My son is in the county jail, and he has bond court tomorrow morning. We already talked to a lawyer, and his bond should be around fifteen thousand, so he gave me your location to see if you could help out."

"Sorry, I can't. I have a lot going on now and don't have money to spare," I said, attempting to walk away.

"Man, I told him about fucking these cornball bitches," she blurted out.

I charged toward her. "Excuse me?"

"Excuse what, lil' girl? I said what I said, shit! Chris always talking to me about how much he's in love with you and how you a real boss-ass bitch. He be praising you, but to me you look like a bitch that's folding."

"Well, it's funny to me that he's telling you all this, but he never mentioned you to me."

"Look, lil' girl, his court date is at nine on twenty-sixth and California. You can meet me in front of the court house if you want to help him out. Either way, I'll find a way for my son." She walked off and never looked back.

"Damn, that's a mean bitch," I said as I walked back in the salon.

"What she want?" Miss B said to me as she sized me up and down, making sure I was straight.

"Nothing at all," I lied because Miss B would have a fit if I even considered helping out.

"She wanted something, Jaz. I sat and stared out the window and watched you go back and forth with her. Who is her son that she spoke of? Please, Jaz, don't say that dude that came here with flowers."

"Yes, that's his mom. And his name is Chris."

"She came in here as if that muthafucka was a kid! That's a grown-ass man. Any time a mother is connected to a child that's old like that, get the fuck away from them both." She clapped hands with her client who was agreeing with her.

I finished up with my client and ran out of there so I could make it to class on time. On the ride over, I pondered if I was a down-ass bitch. I wanted to help him out if he was really in love with me, but how did I know if his mean-ass mama was telling any truth? Miss B would never steer me wrong.

"Thanks for joining us, Jaz," the teacher said as I interrupted the class by walking in late and dropping my phone on the floor. I was so discombobulated. I felt like coming to class was a bad idea and I should have just gone home. There was so much on my mind.

Chris's mom had me really feeling bad for not helping out. As ignorant as she was, I shouldn't have cared, but I did like Chris. As I sat in class, I kept looking at my phone, wishing the jail number would pop back up. I wanted to hear Chris confirm what his mama was talking about with all this love shit. He never told me himself that he loved me, and how could he when we barely knew each other?

I desperately wanted a man to love me, and from so many conversations, Chris reminded me of my father. Damn, if he loved me like she said he did, hell yeah I would help him out. I wanted that type of hood love because I needed somebody down in my life like that. After scribbling both of our names a thousand times on my notebook while not paying attention to the teacher, I made my mind up. I was going to go to that court tomorrow to get my man out.

"Jaz, are you here?" the teacher said as he walked up on me.

"Yes, damn why you so close?" I responded back, making the whole class chuckle. The teacher tapped the board with his extended ruler to grab the class's attention.

"Just a reminder the final exam is tomorrow at 10 a.m. sharp."

"Fuck!" I blurted.

"Please watch your mouth or leave." The teacher was not happy with me today.

"I'm sorry."

"OK, class is dismissed. Enjoy your evening and please study to be ready for tomorrow."

I took a deep breath, relieved to be out of that class. I rushed home to try to figure out what I wanted to do. My phone finally started to vibrate, and I was ecstatic because it was Chris. After pressing one, my baby's voice came through the phone.

"Hey, bae," were his first words.

"Your mama came ambushing my shop today."

"Wow. I know she can be a bit much, but she don't mean no harm. I'm her only son."

A bit much was right, but I didn't want to spend whatever time we had left talking about his bitch-ass mother.

"Bae, you are all right?"

"Yeah, I'm cool."

"Did you think about helping me out? I can get your bread back to you in under a week once I get out of here."

"That's a lot of money, Chris."

"G. Come on, na. I ran across your bank statements. You have more than enough to help me out."

"What?" I was heated by him confirming what I already knew.

"I ran across them while I was heating up some food that night—"

I had to cut him off quick. "You mean when you went rambling through my shit?"

"Mannn," he sang with anger but caught his temper quickly. "Jaz, can you please do this solid for me? I'm going to get your money back ASAP. You know you're my boo. I have fallen deeply in love with you. I've never been around someone so ambitioius as you and someone that makes me want to reach higher for success. You are the perfect woman."

Damn, I thought to myself as I listened to him woo me for a few more minutes. Everything about this felt wrong, but I thought, *Hell, I'm grown, I can do what I want.*

"I got you, baby," I assured him.

"I knew you were a down-ass bitch. I got the right one, and when I get out I'm going to show you everything."

"Bae, the only thing is I can't come up there tomorrow. I got something important to do around the same time."

"Damn, more important than me?"

Hell, yeah! I thought.

"It's not like that, Chris."

"I know, and I love you. It's going to be us against the world on some Bonnie and Clyde shit. That actually works out perfect because my mom is the only one who can bond me out, so you can just give her the money."

"Can I give your mom a check?"

"No, baby, it has to be cash."

"What?" I asked.

"Yes, cash only. I can have my mom come through and scoop the cash. We only have one minute left on the phone, bae."

"Just have her meet me back at the shop in an hour. I have to run to the bank."

"OK, bae, I'm about to call and tell her. I love you so much and can't wait for you to bounce on this dick tomorrow."

Before I could even say *I love you* back, the phone hung up.

I ran out to hit up the bank and meet his mom. Although the *cash only* didn't sit right with me, I made a promise to Chris. So I would deal with his mom; anything to get him back to me.

I sat on the boutique side of the salon for almost thirty minutes waiting on Tracy.

She had the nerve to pull up to my salon, honking her horn like she was crazy. I stepped outside and directed her to

TYPICAL CHI SH*T

come inside but she rolled down the window and screamed, "Girl, c'mon, I got to go."

This old bitch was really working my nerves. I really didn't want to hand her a white envelope full of cash through her passenger-side window, but what choice did I have now? Before she pulled off in her small red Benz, she did say, "Thanks," which in my mother's eyes was a sign of disrespect. My mother always taught me to say "thank you" and only accept that. The short versions were like saying, "Yeah, thanks, bitch."

Every day I lived my life, I always remembered something my mother said. I was very appreciative of those thoughts. As I locked the boutique up and headed to my car, it finally sank in that I just handed that evil bitch fifteen thousand dollars in cash.

CHAPTER 10

"FIFTEEN THOUSAND DOLLARS! Fifteen stacks!" I repeated after I took a shot of Patrón. Shit, I had to switch from dark liquor to something stronger a few days ago. I didn't even know Chris's mom to hand over that much cash—to be honest, I barely knew Chris. Hell, what the fuck was I thinking? That's the problem: I wasn't thinking at all. If my mama could see me, I know for sure she would slap me into the middle of next week. This was the type of guy she warned me about.

I had been beating myself for days now, thinking of them scamming-ass people. I thought I was smarter than this. How could I be so dumb and naïve? "Fuck!" I screamed after I took another shot of Patrón. My throat was actually starting to burn; I had to grab a bottle of water to cool it down.

TYPICAL CHI SH*T

This is exactly why I needed my mama—for stupid adult mistakes. I probably would've been away at college with corny college dudes by now if my mom were still alive, but instead, I ended up with a fraud-ass son of a bitch.

I'd been trying to contact Chris for days. I had two phone numbers for him, but both numbers were disconnected. I never asked him his last name, so I couldn't check the county system to see if he was released. I didn't have his mother's number to call her, and even if I did, she probably wouldn't talk to me. I'd circled neighborhoods looking for him, especially South Chicago Street where we met. I bet Britt would know how to find him, but I wouldn't dare reach out to her.

How could I fuck someone and not know their last name? I questioned myself day and night for making that dumb mistake. I really thought he loved me. I really messed up. I was furious.

After that bottle of water, I relaxed back on the couch in complete silence, still in deep thought but becoming calm now. I had almost fallen to sleep but I was startled by a knock at the door. Who the fuck could have made it past my doorman? I looked in the direction of my room where my purse was that held my gun.

"Open up, Jaz. I can hear you in there." It was David's voice.

Of course, I didn't want to open the door, but I didn't want my neighbors to think anything negative of me if I screamed what I really wanted to say out the door.

"Man, what the fuck you want?" was the first thing I said as I opened the door.

"I'm sorry, Jaz! I'm sorry. Please forgive me," he begged.

"Forgive you?" I said with so much anger.

David wanted to stand right there and talk, but I wanted to fight. I wanted to slap him upside his head so many times. I actually reached toward him and he grabbed my hand and proceeded to hug me while still whispering in my ear, "I'm sorry, Jaz."

I broke loose and took a good look at him now, standing in my living room looking like a sad puppy. David had lost so much weight. He went from his high school athletic body to tall and slim. I guess it was true what they say about college kids. They starve.

"I know we weren't official, David, but really? You fucked Britt, out of all people?" I blurted.

"Jaz, if you knew how sorry I was. I'm even sorry for sleeping with you."

"What?" I was confused.

"Yes. I miss your body, I do, but most importantly I miss our friendship and our talks. Everything about us is fucked up, and that shit eats me alive."

Damn, I felt the same way. It ate me up not having my best friend around. I just sat there and stared at him.

"Jaz, is there any way I can make this up to you? I really want my friend back," he pleaded.

"How could you be so stupid? How could you not notice

she was out to hurt me? Do you think she wanted your stupid ass?"

"Jaz. I haven't been eating or sleeping right, and I'm barely passing my classes."

"So, am I supposed to feel sorry for you?" I asked, looking him straight in his eyes.

"No, I'm not asking for your sympathy. I'm here to apologize."

He tried to grab my arm and pull me close, but I snatched it away.

"Bye, David. I've been happy these last few weeks, and I don't need you around me."

"If you're so happy, why are your eyes red? Why is your face breaking out?" he said. He stared into my eyes. "You have the most beautiful skin until you get stressed."

David was right; he knew me too well. These past few days of anger at Chris had stressed me out, and my face was horrible. I hated that David was right. I wasn't going to let him know how right he was. My head was hurting and I was ready for him to go. He had made himself comfortable on my couch as if I had accepted him back in my life.

A thought came to me about using David to help me find Chris. I wanted my muthafuckin' money back. I knew David knew more about the streets than I did; furthermore, he was still close with Britt, and she for damn sure knew where Chris hung out.

As I sat at my counter and attempted to get rid of my headache with hot tea, it dawned on me that my headache would never leave if I let David keep rumbling on about how sorry he was. My last nerve was struck and he had to get out.

"David, you have to go now. I need to rest," I said as I walked over to the door.

"You can't fool me; we've been friends since fifth grade. I know you more than you know you."

"If you know me so well, David, why didn't you know not to hurt me? Together or not, we were fucking every damn day! The moment you left, you had the audacity to fuck Britt!"

David started walking toward me with the most pitiful look, but before he could reach me, I screamed, "Why are you here? I don't need this emotional-ass shit right now."

"I wanted to see you. I wanted to hug you. I wanted to apologize to your face, and I know you will never forgive me, but I do want you to be my friend again. Jaz, I will do anything I can to make this up to you."

My eyebrows rose. "Anything?" I asked. I knew exactly what he could do to make it up to me.

"Yes, Jaz," he said as he walked closer to my face.

I looked David directly in his eyes and let the words roll right off my tongue. "Kill someone for me, David." As shocked as I was in that moment, the words had come out and I couldn't take them back.

CHAPTER 11

"WHAT THE FUCK, Jaz, are you serious?" David said as he started walking in circles around me. He chanted, "Murder? Murder, Jaz?"

I grabbed David's shoulder as he circled around me in distress, scratching his head.

"I'm just playing," I blurted, but I knew it was too late.

"No, the hell you're not."

"David, would you please calm down? You said you would do anything! That was just a test," I said, trying to convince him that I wasn't serious. "Do you want a bottle of water, juice, or tea? Please have something. You are making me nervous."

"A test? Are you fucking kidding me? What the fuck is going on? Did someone hurt you? Why would you joke about some shit like that?"

"Damn, David, I was just playing."

"*Damn, David*, my ass," he spat before walking out the door.

The door slammed, and all I could say was *damn*. I couldn't believe that came out my mouth. I hoped he wouldn't go vent to no one about this. His face was fucked up. I'd never seen David that mad before. I bit my lip, feeling guilty for asking him to do some shit like that. He kept asking me what he could do to make up for his betrayal, and that's the only thing I wanted: for Chris to be found and dead.

Blood money was all I had left of my mom. It was insurance money, but it took my mom bleeding out and dying for me to get it. This money caused me pain and distance from people I thought were my friends. I was scammed out of a great portion of it by Chris, and that ate me up inside. He fucking finessed me, but I would get the last laugh—that was for sure. I was headed out the house today to hit a few more blocks just to see if I would bump into him. Chicago was small, and he couldn't hide forever.

As I soaked in a hot bath, thinking of all the wrong happening in my life, tears fell from my eyes. My eyes had permanent bags from my constant crying.

It was like a light popped in my head when I realized I needed to boss the fuck up. Every situation that I got myself in, I always thought of what my mother would do. I knew damn well she wouldn't be crying every damn day.

I got out the bathtub with suds running down my legs.

After wrapping my towel around my wet body, I sat inside my walk-in closet, deciding what I would wear tomorrow to take on this evil-ass world. "No more distractions, Jaz," I said to myself as I looked in my vanity mirror.

My phone started to ring in the bedroom, and I contemplated going to get it.

After it stopped ringing, it started back within seconds. "Shit, it could be Chris," I said as I rushed to the bedroom before it stopped ringing again.

As I looked at the phone, I thought, *What do I say? Fuck it.* I might as well let her have it.

"What the fuck do you want?" I howled as I picked up.

"Jaz, my bad."

"Your bad? " I repeated. "That's all you got to say?"

"Seriously, I'm sorry," Britt said through my phone.

"Sorry? You are just as sorry as they come."

"Wow, Jaz, you sure do know how to hit below the belt."

"Well, if the shoe fits, lace it up, bitch!" I screamed through the phone.

Britt took a deep breath, and there it was ... all the hate that she had for me came pouring out her mouth like water from a damn faucet. "Jaz, you've always thought you were better than me. Shit, you thought you were better than the entire school because you had money and sympathy."

"Sympathy?" I was confused.

"Yes, bitch, sympathy! In fifth grade, your granny died, so everybody felt bad for Jaz. Then in eighth grade, your dad died right before graduation, so fuck everybody; it was all about Jaz. Let's not forget when we got to high school and your mom opened her little business and became popular in my neighborhood—because you didn't live there. Y'all were up in that nice neighborhood but came on back to help out the poor folks. You always thought you were better. Every tragedy gave you more money or more power."

"What are you talking about? You sound dumb. You pop up to my event and act an ass, then you go away to school and fuck the only person I was close to."

"Yeah, I fucked David because I've always wanted to and because I knew you were secretly fucking him. The only way to get the truth was to do what I did. You can't have everything, Jaz. The world doesn't revolve around you."

"You are sick. You have been a jealous friend since fifth grade and just stringing along to collect whatever you can."

"Collect, bitch?"

"Yes! You have been a free-loading bitch, always using people. I've seen you use a lot of people. I should've known you weren't a real friend any damn way. We were never friends. It was just the time we'd known each other keeping us together."

"Bitch, I fucked your man because you lied! You always wanted to be private but had your ears wide open to other people's mess, always judging, thinking you were better, and that's why I made sure Chris took you for some of that cash. You are so dumb to the streets; you an easy lick and I just hit your ass."

This bitch had the nerve to hang up on my face. I

couldn't believe what she just said, so I dialed Britt right back but the phone went to voicemail. I tried sending a text, but it never got delivered; this bitch had blocked me. Unlike with Chris, I knew where she was at. I grabbed my shoes after throwing on some joggers and headed straight to the door. I was about to drive four hours to her school and beat this bitch. As soon as I opened the door, I was startled.

"What the fuck are you doing here?"

The words came out his mouth: "I'll do it, Jaz. I'll kill whoever. I just want to be with you forever."

CHAPTER 12

DAVID GRABBED MY arm and rushed me back into my place. He started kissing me, and I was feeling him. I couldn't believe my ears, as my soul was happy to finally have someone who was ready to kill for me because Lord knows, I couldn't do it myself. The argument with Britt was pushed to the back of my mind; I needed to enjoy this moment with David. We kissed right by the door for what felt like an hour, but I know it was shorter. David pulled down my joggers and ran right in me from behind. He was taking charge, and I wasn't used to him in this way. He must have missed this ass as much as I missed his dick. I'd never felt David's dick like this before; he was pounding and grabbing my hair, but as usual it was over in a matter of moments.

"Whew, I missed you so much, Jaz," he said as he pulled his pants up and sat back on the couch.

My pussy was still pounding and craving more dick, and his ass was already comfortable on the couch with the remote control in his hand. I pulled my pants up and sat across from him on the other couch.

"Bring that ass over here. Come sit on my lap and let's talk business."

I went to the kitchen to grab bottles of water for our cottonmouth. We could barely catch our breath.

"Thanks. Now tell me what's going on, or you can just tell me what I got to do."

"Damn, are you serious?"

"Hell yeah! I hurt you, and I want to prove to you that you can trust me again. I want you to know that I'm never leaving your side," David said before he kissed me again.

I wanted to enjoy this moment of feeling loved, so I just laid back in his arms as he flipped through the channels on the television. We eventually fell asleep right there in each other's arms. The couch was uncomfortable, but I refused to move because I hadn't relaxed this well in weeks.

The next morning, I was surprised that I had slept until nine. I was also surprised to find David staring at me.

"Good morning, sleepy head," David said, staring me straight in my eyes.

I hopped up, not sure what was going on. I starting throwing pillows everywhere in a panic. "Where is my phone?" I repeated several times.

"Jaz, calm down. What's wrong?"

"Nothing. I just need my phone."

"Your phone is in the kitchen somewhere. It was ringing, but I didn't want to wake you."

"What? You let me sleep while my phone was ringing? Why would you do that?"

"I'm sorry. You were sleeping so peacefully and snoring so hard, I couldn't dare wake you up."

I grabbed my phone, praying it was Chris calling, but it was just two missed calls from Miss B, who I had been ignoring for several days.

"Is everything all right, Jaz? I think it's time to tell me what's going on."

"OK, but can I take a shower first?"

"Sure, and I'll get something started for us to eat. Or do you want to go out to grab something at a restaurant?"

"Nah, I miss your cooking."

"That's all you miss about me?" David said as he held up a box of pancake mix.

"Yes, sir," I joked.

"Shit, can I use your laptop?"

"Yes, but what's wrong?"

"I need to email my counselor at the school about dropping my classes."

"What? Why would you do that?"

"You need someone to protect you, and I'm that person."

"Wow," I said, leaning into him for a hug.

I walked away slowly, wishing he would follow me into the bathroom to finish what we started yesterday, but when I looked back at him he was headed toward the kitchen.

As I was in the shower, I contemplated if I should even tell David what was going on. Of course, I wanted my revenge and my money back. But did I want David to get involved? How else could he prove his loyalty to me? I had no one else to consider helping me take down Chris. One thing was for certain: Chris was going down, and he was going down soon.

CHAPTER 13

"WOAH, LOOK WHO decided to walk back in here from the dead," Miss B said as she popped her gum and spun her chair. Although she was older, she was stuck in her around-the-way girl stage. She always had a long ponytail to the side, and she wore bamboo earrings. Miss B reminded me of my mom in so many ways. When I'm down, I stay away from her because she can see right through me.

"Miss B, please give me a break."

"Give you a break? Yeah, I'm going to break my foot right in your ass. You had me in here, collecting your booth rent and working the boutique side of the place while you was probably somewhere laying up, having sex."

"It wasn't like that. I just needed time to get myself together. Damn."

"Don't *damn* me because you fed me that story some

days ago. You need to boss the fuck up!" M．
handed me an envelope full of cash.

I walked away, counting the money, trying not
any attention to Miss B.

"Heyyyyy, Jaz," an unfamiliar voice sang.

"Hey, girl!" I pretended to know her as I kept walking toward the boutique side of the salon. The face was familiar, but I had no idea where I knew her from; she was too young to be a classmate of mine.

I decided to send David a thank-you text for breakfast and for making sure I got rest. *Thank God,* I thought because we never got to have the conversation about Chris. Although David told me he was dropping his classes for me, I knew he had to help his mom with his younger sisters by the way he ran out the door after breakfast.

"Hey, Jaz, you mind if I look at any of your dresses?" the young girl said as she touched on everything.

"Sure, girl. Can you remind me where I know you from again?"

"The bowling alley. I was your server when you were there with the big guy a few weeks ago, and I commented on your sunglasses. You showed me where to find them at. You remember me now?"

"Oh yeah. I remember."

"This city is so small. Who would've known you worked with my aunt?"

"Who is your aunt?"

ing back toward her aunt,

...orld."

...e bowling, I'm going to give you ...ily discount. My aunt said you are like a ...o her, so that makes us cousins, right?" She giggled in the sweetest voice.

"Right. I'm going to visit you soon and find you a dress in here. You can have it for free; just shout out my boutique on your social media."

"Aw, thank you, Jaz! But let me warn you not to come on Sundays," she said with a goofy grin.

"Why the warning?"

"That heavy dude you was with that time I saw you—he be there with his wife and kids. I don't want you in no drama, new cousin." She laughed again as she proceeded to look through the inventory.

I was appalled. I'd been looking for this bastard, and he was right up the street from my house? And did she say *his kids and a wife*? I was livid. I tossed the envelope of cash in my purse and walked out the door to call David.

"Babe, pull up on me at the shop ASAP," I said in a panic as soon as David picked up the phone.

David hung up without saying a word. I knew he was on his way.

The type of energy David was giving me felt like the shit he did was worth it. I hated that he had to do it with Britt, but I couldn't focus on her anymore. I had real problems now. Not only did Chris run off with my money—he had a wife and kids that he never mentioned to me.

"Son of a bitch!" I screamed in the car before punching my steering wheel, making the horn go off and drawing attention from inside the shop. Just as I expected, Miss B ran her nosy ass out.

"Jaz, why are you blowing the horn and why are you sitting in the car? This is the hood. This ain't that fancy neighborhood you live in."

"I'm waiting on David to pull up."

"David?" Miss B held her hand over her head.

"I'll be back inside in a moment." I tried to shoot Miss B away before David pulled up because I didn't need her in our conversation.

I let my seat back in the car to try to collect my thoughts. David needed to know that what we were about to do was for my money and not about the lies Chris's bitch-ass told me.

David pulled up so fast that he almost knocked off my side mirror. He caused unnecessary attention by slamming my door. I prayed Miss B didn't storm back out the shop, thinking it was a problem.

"What's up, Jaz?" David said, staring me down.

"I'm fine. What are you looking for?"

"You called me in such a panic. I thought you were hurt."

"No, I just think it's time we talk about what's really going on."

"Go ahead. I'm listening."

"David, I was messing around with Chris and—"

"Chris? The fat muthafucka that showed up to your grand opening with Britt?"

"Yes," I said with a shameful face. I wished he could just kill him without me getting into details. He would be upset that I loved every inch of that big scamming muthafucka.

"What did he do to you?"

"Well, long story short—him and his mama basically bullied me out of some cash."

"How much cash?"

"Fifteen K," I mumbled.

"Fifteen fucking thousand dollars?"

"Yes," I said with my head leaning on the steering wheel.

The car was silent for a moment then I blurted out, "I would have never got serious with him if you wouldn't have fucked Britt." That was a lie, but I needed David to feel bad and not feel like he could question me for my bad decisions. I wanted David to focus on what was important.

"Damn, Jaz."

"Look, if you want to back out, then be my guest. I can do this myself."

"Do what yourself? You talk a good game, but you've never committed a crime in your life. You only had one fight in your entire life because Britt fought all your battles."

"Don't you ever say that bitch's name in my presence! That bitch set this up to happen! She sent that bastard after my money."

David's face blew up like a bull blowing smoke. "Britt

did what? That bitch is unbelievable. Aight, where this fucker at?"

"I just found out where he hangs out on Sundays."

"Good, I'm going to shoot that muthafucka."

"David, we need a solid plan so we can move past this." I tried to calm David by rubbing his hand.

He was still hyper. "Fuck that! I will kill him and Britt!"

"Britt, babe?" I had to question.

"Yes! That bitch put that muthafucka in your life, so she got to go too."

"No, babe, I'll handle her with an ass whooping. I got her, trust me."

"You know damn well you can't win a fight with Britt," David said, laughing.

The tension was cut by the laughter but we still had a plan to put in motion. Now that I knew where Chris was, I just needed to check things out.

"Excuse me, Jaz," Miss B said as she tapped on the passenger's side of the window, startling David.

With the way David jumped, I needed to re-think if he could really kill Chris.

"I'm coming inside now, Miss B."

"Yeah, come inside. You have stuff everywhere." Miss B signaled me to hurry up.

David and I got out the car. He reached to kiss me, but I walked off slowly because Miss B was watching and that was a conversation I didn't want to explain. She had a rule of never forgiving a guy that cheated. That's probably why she was in her forties and single because she was definitely too pretty not to have a thousand guys crawling over her.

"Thank you for the pieces. I'm going to make sure I promote your boutique." The young girl made her way back to me with her fresh sew-in with tight curls.

"What's your name again, boo?"

"Tasha."

"OK, Tasha. I'm going to come up to see you at the bowling alley soon."

"Yes, girl! Come tonight. It's Wednesday, so three-dollar bowl. It be slow—just a lot of older people taking advantage of the special. I can get you a lane for free tonight. I'm on my way there now until ten."

"OK, cool. I'm going to slide."

I sat down in the chair by the register and really started to think of a plan on how to catch Chris. It dawned on me that I should actually slide to the bowling alley tonight just to peep the scene. I needed to know how many cameras were actually there and how many cameras were in the parking garage. I needed to do all the footwork so it could be easy for David to pull the trigger.

CHAPTER 14

AS SOON AS I walked in the bowling alley, I couldn't help but think about being there with Chris. I was goofy enough to fall for him. Every time I thought of him, I only got more pissed off. I wasn't sure if I was madder about the money or mad at myself for thinking a guy could love me so quick.

"Hello, how can I help you?" a guy with a red-collared shirt that had a Strikes Bowling logo on it asked.

"I'm looking for Tasha?"

"She hasn't made it here yet, but I can assist you with a lane if you want me to."

"Sure, that would be fine."

I thought Tasha would be here to give me a discount, but it was only three dollars to bowl and three dollars for shoes. I decided it would be the perfect time to get some practice in so it wouldn't look suspicious with me just walking around, looking at cameras.

When I walked over to my lane, I saw balloons and a kid on lane seven. I hated that the lanes were so damn close. Now I had to be a part of a little kid's party. As I started to bowl, I was minding my business, hitting my strikes, not even paying those bad, loud-ass kids any mind. I had two strikes back to back and was headed for strike number three, which would've been my first turkey ever.

As I was getting my posture right, I heard a familiar voice. "Happy birthday, baby girl!"

"Thanks, Daddy!" a young girl said.

I turned around. It was Chris.

I definitely didn't get the strike. I guttered the muthafuckin' ball. I looked his fat ass dead in the eye but couldn't say a word. I was speechless, stuck. I'd played this scene out in my head a thousand times. I couldn't believe my mouth wouldn't move. The same little girl who had called him Daddy ran toward me to retrieve a toy she'd dropped. I kicked that damn toy so hard; it almost hit my next strike for me. He had the nerve to walk his ass over to me and tell his daughter, "Go back to your friends. Daddy will get the toy."

He looked at me as if he didn't even know me. I wanted to put on a scene. I wanted to be rude and disrespectful, but the G in me kept cool.

As many times as I practiced in the mirror about what

would be said and done, I couldn't believe I choked up like a little bitch.

I sprinted off toward my car and saw Tasha rushing in to work, but I just kept moving past her. As I started walking into the garage, I heard his fat ass calling my name and scooting up on me. If he were smaller, he would've been running, but his ass couldn't move that fast.

"Jaz! Stop, Jaz. Goddamn, would you slow down?"

I turned around, charging toward him. He caught my arms and held them tight. I started crying and falling, being all dramatic and shit. He picked me up then whispered in my ear, "I have my reasons for staying away from you, please forgive me."

"Where the fuck is my money, Chris? Britt already told me she led you to setting me up. Give me my money and this can be squashed today. Or else."

"Excuse me? Or else, what?"

I got quiet because I didn't mean to say that. Chris's face changed completely.

"Or else what, Jaz? I don't do good with threats, so if you want to do something, do it."

I turned around and started walking off when I felt Chris's hand on the back of my neck.

"Look, bitch, I was trying to be nice to your nerd-ass, but if you ever spit a threat out your mouth toward me again, I'll kill you. Whatever you thinking, you better think twice about it. You can forget about that punk-ass fifteen thousand dollars that's gone. You weren't shit but a sweet lick."

He let my neck go and walked off, and that's when I noticed a security cop circling the garage. I wanted to flag him down, but I could hardly catch my breath. I rushed to the car to tell David about what happened. Although I knew this would drive David crazy, I just had to tell him now.

"David, he hit me!" I screamed in the phone.

"Who hit you? Where are you? What are you talking about?" David rushed me with questions.

"Chris hit me."

"What? Where are you, Jaz?"

"I'm downtown in the Strikes parking lot."

"Stay there. I'm leaving from in front of your crib now."

David hung up the phone and I could only imagine how fast he was driving to get to me.

I was nervous and shaking in the front seat of my car. As I looked out my window, I saw Chris walking in the garage toward a tinted black Jeep. I slid down so he wouldn't see me, but I could hear his voice as he talked on his phone.

"Yo friend a fucking psycho. I had to get that bitch together at the bowling alley."

I didn't know who he was talking to, but I could only imagine it was Britt.

I didn't hear his voice anymore; I just heard the loud pipes from the Jeep then it skirted off.

Oh hell no, I thought. He was not about to get away from me. I started to follow the Jeep and as we pulled out,

I saw David speeding down Michigan Ave. in the opposite direction of us. He must have seen me as well because my phone started ringing.

"Where are you going?" David yelled in the phone.

"I'm following Chris. He's in front of me in the Jeep with the dark tinted windows."

David said nothing, but he hung up.

I continued to follow Chris as he hopped on Lake Shore Drive expressway. I was keeping up in my old model Benz truck that was once my mom's and was now mine. It had started to drizzle and I normally would have driven slow in the rain, but I had to keep up. We crossed over to the Dan Ryan expressway, and that's when I saw David's car zoom right past me. I thought he was going to flag Chris down to talk shit, but within seconds I heard the sound of three gunshots.

POW POW POW

My eyes closed for a second. It was as if I wasn't on the expressway. "Thank God," I said to myself because I was able to make a instant stop. The rain had everyone driving slower than usual and that was perfect because I could have ended up in a ditch.

The Jeep had lost control and spun around at least five times before crashing into a wall; there was smoke coming from under the hood as if the car was about to blow. Other cars were slowing down to look at the scene. One man got out to actually help, and that's when I noticed Chris getting out of the passenger's side, bent over and holding his stomach with blood dripping from his head. Chris was screaming as he made his way over to the driver's side. When he got the door open, he suddenly collapsed to the ground. By now, several cars had stopped and everyone's attention was on the person in the driver's seat. I couldn't see from my position, but if David didn't shoot Chris, who did he hit?

CHAPTER 15

MY PHONE HAD started ringing and the rain started to come down heavy on my windshield. I was sitting there, still in shock. Several cars had stopped now; I had no choice but to drive away so I could get to a safe location to grab my phone. It had fallen under the seat from my sudden stop. I had so many questions to ask David. I finally pulled myself together and started driving around the cars. I could hear the police sirens coming. I got off the expressway, but I couldn't see who was in that driver's seat. I needed to know who was hurt or dead. Who did David actually shoot?

I needed to catch my breath fast because I couldn't drive another block without knowing what was going on with David. I made an exit on thirty-fifth street, which was right by my salon. I spotted David's car as soon as I pulled onto the block. His lights were off, but his engine was still running; I could see the smoke coming from the tail pipe. When I rushed over to the car, David was crying. David still had the gun in his hand and was shaking.

"What did I do, Jaz?" he said with tears falling from his eyes.

I had no choice but to take charge of the situation. David couldn't function, and I knew it would only be moments before the cops started looking for David's car. I wanted to break down with David, but I was taught to stay strong no matter what. My friend was weeping and trembling, my heart was shattered, and I never meant to drag David into this. All of this was a reaction to love, hate, and money.

"David, my car is running and my house keys are in there. Please pull yourself together and drive to my house. I will get rid of the car and the gun," I said as I took my jacket off to wrap the gun in it. I remembered my daddy slapping me in the face when I was a kid just for picking up his gun. That was the only time my father had ever hit me. I was angry until my mother explained that I should never touch a gun that wasn't mine.

David got out his car, and he could barely walk. I gave him a tight hug and whispered in his ear, "I got us."

I sat in the driver's seat of David's car with no clue what to do first. I watched David finally pull off in my car after stalling for about five minutes. "Shit!" I screamed as I hit the steering wheel. I was a nervous wreck myself. I noticed a weird smell and looked on the passenger's seat—David's vomit was just sitting there. "Jaz, pull yourself together," I said to myself as I pulled off, heading south with no clue where I was going.

Tears fell from my eyes. I had no one to call; the only person I ever relied on—besides my parents—was David. And now with him being fucked up, I had no one. I had been driving for hours, and now my eyes were beginning to close. I was tired and didn't know how much longer I could drive. After a truck honked at me and flashed his lights, scaring the shit out of me, I knew I had to pull to the side. I noticed I was on a bridge over water. I thought I would get out and drop the gun in the water. It was something I'd seen in movies a million times.

As easy as it was to throw the gun over the bridge, I wished I could throw the car over as well. When I returned to the inside of the car, I noticed that the car was off, which was strange because I left it running. I tried turning the key, but the car wouldn't start. I repeated it about five times and still nothing. I couldn't believe I didn't have my phone or my purse; I was not thinking clearly when I jumped in this car. Damn, if it wasn't one thing it was another. I had no choice but to start walking to the nearest exit. I had cars pulling over, asking if I wanted a ride, and trucks kept honking at me, but I just kept looking straight and praying that God would get me through this. I was cold at first, but after walking so long I heated up fast.

"Thank you, God, thank you, God!" I repeated out loud

as I saw a sign that said this exit was for Southern Illinois University.

What a relief, I thought. If only I could make it to the college. I had plenty of homies there, including Monica. Britt was there as well, but I prayed I wouldn't see her face. The sun was really out now. My Apple watch had died, and I had no clue what time it was or where exactly to go. I was relieved that I was closer to someone now than I was an hour ago.

As I walked past a gas station, I wished I had money to get a bottle of water because my mouth was dry as cotton.

"Jaz, is that you?" I heard a girl say, and when I turned around it was Monica pumping her gas.

"OMG, Monica!" I screamed and ran toward her, reaching for a hug.

"Jaz, what are you doing here—walking? You look and smell bad. What the fuck?" Monica questioned. Monica didn't hold anything back, as I expected; she always spoke her mind.

Desperately, I asked, "Where are you headed?"

"I'm headed back to the city. My parents are moving and I wanted to pack my own room up because my dad would just throw out all my shit."

"Please, can I catch a ride with you back home?" I begged.

"Sure, get in."

I started to cry as I got inside Monica's car. I couldn't believe what I'd just been through. I laid the seat back and rubbed my thighs to get some feeling back into them. Monica jumped right on the expressway and headed north. I knew it wouldn't be long before she started to ask questions, so I closed my eyes and pretended to sleep.

Monica had Drake blasting loud and she was speeding on the highway; the faster, the better for me. I was still trying to grasp every emotion that was going through my body then I felt the car slowing down.

"What the fuck?" Monica screamed over the music.

I peeped one eye open to see what was going on, and there it was across the highway: David's car struck by a semi truck. Everybody on our side was riding slow, looking at it. The police and an ambulance were across the way.

"Drive, nosy muthafuckas!" Monica screamed out her window while laying on the horn of the car.

By now, I had sat up completely. I had to keep my eyes on her because I didn't make it this far to die in the car with this road-rage-having bitch.

"Damn, that looks like David's car," Monica looked at me and said.

"I didn't see it." I tried to play dumb, but I knew damn well that was his car.

"Should I turn around and double-check—"

"No!" I screamed.

"Damn, OK, Jaz, relax."

CHAPTER 16

"JAZ, WAKE UP," Monica said as she was hitting my legs.

I could barely see straight. The sun was shining bright through the window.

"Where do you want me to drop you off at?"

"Drop me off? Damn, we're back in the city that fast?"

"Girl, yes, and you were snoring down. It's been almost five hours."

"Thank you, Monica. I really appreciate the ride. You can drop me off at my shop. I owe you, G. You came through in the clutch for me."

"Yeah, you owe me the truth, starting with how the hell you ended up damn near five hours away from home, walking up a highway ramp and smelling like horse shit."

"I don't want to talk about it."

"You got to tell me something, Jaz."

I needed something quick to tell this bitch because she was not about to let this go. And this was the most talkative bitch in the city, so my story needed to be air tight.

"OK, if you really want to know, I was driving to free my mind. I've still been pissed about Britt and David, so I headed toward your school, thinking I could run into them."

"Why would you be pissed about Britt and David? That wasn't your man. Or was it?"

"Yeah, he was something like that."

"Bitch, this tea is hot!"

"Whatever. So, yeah, basically I was coming down there to find Britt."

"So what happened?"

"My car stopped on the highway and after it was towed, I was so pissed and wanted to just walk."

"Damn, G, that was dangerous. You did all this for love?"

"Yeah, Monica."

"G, we thought you were a good girl, all single and shit. And your sneaky ass was fucking with the boy everybody wanted."

I chuckled to keep my composure because I was falling apart inside. I was relieved to see that we were finally pulling up to my salon—although the shop was full of people, which was normal for noon on a Thursday.

I had a problem: I couldn't go in the shop looking like this because Miss B would give me the third degree. My body was screaming for a hot shower.

"Thanks, Monica. I really appreciate you. Please try to keep this between you and I."

"Now, girl, you know I ain't going to tell nobody."

I smirked before I got out the car because I knew she was about to get on the phone with somebody as soon I closed the door.

When I got out the car, my head was down. I couldn't believe I was about to walk in my place of business smelling and looking this, but I had to get a phone so I could get me an Uber to check on David.

It was the end of October. Chicago was brisk and sunny. Our days were unpredictable; one day it would be sunny and sixty, but the next day it would be liable to snow. I heard a honk just as I was about to walk in the salon door.

It was David. I flew to the corner where he was sitting in my car. I knew Miss B might have got a glimpse of me because her work station was right in front, but I'd rather her nag at me than actually smell the filth on my body.

"Jaz, are you OK?" David was rubbing my face.

I fell into his arms and started crying. The last twenty-four hours were such a rush, and my body was tired. When I was finally able to let loose, I couldn't say a word. David kissed my face.

"Jaz, I didn't kill Chris."

"I know because Chris was on the passenger's side when you shot through the driver's side window. Who did you kill?"

"No one."

I was confused. "No one? Who told you that? Where have you been? What's going on?"

"Calm down, babe, that's a lot of questions."

"Calm down? Do you know what I've been through these last couple of hours with that gun and your car?" I was desperate to know what was going on.

"I'm sorry, baby, but this is what I found out from the news and social media. I haven't been to sleep, either. I've been up at your place all night, pacing the floor and watching TV. Someone actually had some of the scene on Facebook. Chris had one of his guys driving, and I grazed him in the neck and shot him once in the arm. The news said he was in critical condition last night, but he's stable now. Most of the trauma came from the head injury caused by the accident."

"That's good news!" I said with excitement, but David was not as happy.

"What's wrong?"

"Let's just go to your crib. I been on this block for four hours waiting on you to pop up. I noticed you left your phone and purse in your car."

David pulled off. First, we were quiet, but I could see from the side of David's face that he was worried about something. As much as I wanted to question him, I just couldn't take on anything else right now. My soul itself was relieved that no one died. My body was tired.

It didn't take long for us to get to my house. As soon as I hit the door, I rushed to my bathroom to clean my body.

I needed a hot bath desperately. I started some bath water with extra bubbles. As my water ran, I couldn't help but stare in the mirror and look at myself. My eyes were weary.

As I soaked in the tub, my mind was racing. I knew this was not the life my mom planned for me. I was nineteen years old with a GED and a business that I had no idea how to run. I had just made myself an accessory to a crime and could possibly face jail time. If my mom and dad were alive, I could just picture me on a college campus with a basketball-star boyfriend. I wondered how a normal life felt. My life was moving fast right now: drugs, liquor, and sex were all I ever craved.

"Lord, if you get us out this mess, I promise to do better," I said out loud, staring at the ceiling as my body soaked. I had to turn our life around. I knew it was my fault that David was even in this mess. He couldn't even look at me in my face straight.

"Jaz, I got you some hot tea," David said as he slowly walked in the bathroom.

"Thank you."

"So, where is my car and gun?"

"I took care of it for us."

"What do you mean, *you took care of it*? Jaz, tell me where is it!" he shouted.

"Damn, David, calm down."

"Jaz, they have my fucking license plate on the news!"

"Damn," I said because I had no other words for him.

"I think I need to turn myself in."

"No!" I hopped up from lying back in the tub.

"Yes, Jaz!"

"What? This is all my fault," I mumbled.

"I'm grown and I reacted too fast when you told me that bastard hit you. I'm taking all this heat."

Tears were falling from my eyes, and I had no words.

"Just promise you will boss up, baby. You have so much potential to be better. Please stop drinking and become the boss that I know you are."

I hopped out the tub with my dripping-wet body. As David stood up, we just hugged tight. I couldn't let go, and we cried together until he started kissing on me.

"I love you, Jaz, and I would appreciate one more night lying next to you. Then tomorrow, I will turn myself in."

"Of course, baby. But you will not be turning yourself in without the best lawyer in the city."

"I can't afford a lawyer, baby."

"David, after everything you've done for me, do you think I would leave you hanging? I have money saved and I would use every penny to help you."

David held me close. "I will never take your money."

"I owe you my life, David," I assured him one last time before pulling him out the bathroom and leading him to the bedroom. I could tell he was nervous about tomorrow and I didn't have the words to help, so I pushed him down on the bed, pulling his pants down.

"What are you doing, Jaz?"

"Shhh," I whispered.

His dick was limp, but after placing it in my mouth and giving it a few warm strokes, it started to rise right down my throat. I started to gag a bit but all the spit created from that I put on the tip of his dick. I looked him in the eyes as he was trying to hold back, but after five seconds of a whirlwind and a lot of spit, he was busting all in my mouth and screaming, "Shit, Jaz, goddamn it!"

I wiped my mouth and lay across the bed where I thought he was going to start snoring as usual. But this time he grabbed my hair and went straight in from behind.

"You thought it was over? If this is my last night with you, then you about to feel every inch of this dick."

We had several breaks in between the sex. Hell, we even lit a blunt.

"Is that a phone ringing?" David asked later.

I hopped up but I could barely walk; my insides were sore. Both of our phones were on the counter and by the time I reached them, they were both ringing. Miss B was calling me and David's mom was calling him.

We snapped back into reality fast. We knew what the calls were about. I could only imagine that David's face was on the news once his license plate came back. Miss B watched the news every hour on the hour. I let David pick up his phone first.

As he answered on speaker, his mom screamed into the phone, "David, what did you do?"

CHAPTER

"MA, CALM DOWN," David said as he paced the floor, naked.

"Where are you? The police were just banging down the door, looking for you. Oh my God, David, what did you do?" David's mom was screaming; we could hear the hurt in her voice. "Jesus, help my boy," she sang on the phone.

"Ma, I'm headed to the police station to turn myself in. Just please calm down."

"Calm down? The police said you shot someone on the expressway. That's attempted murder! What do you mean, *calm down*?"

"Fuuuuuck!" David said as he slid down on the floor.

I grabbed the phone and listened to David's mom cry all while I was looking at David fall apart. I couldn't help but blame myself.

"Hello?" David's mom asked.

"Yes, this is Jaz. I'm calling David a lawyer to go with him to turn himself in."

"We can't afford a lawyer, Jaz."

"I'm paying for it," I assured Ms. Bowens, hoping that would calm her down.

"Is he at your house? I'm on my way."

She hung the phone up and I knew she was headed straight to us. Tears had started falling from David's face, and as much as I wanted to sit down and hug him, I knew I needed to get him some help.

I ran to my room and grabbed a box that kept some of my mom's personal things. I grabbed my mother's old cell phone so I could find a lawyer's number. I knew she had a couple of lawyer friends; I just prayed that one of them could help us. After finding three names that had *lawyer* next to them, I called and left voicemails. One lawyer, Brandon Brown, had two numbers; I texted the one that said *cell* because I needed to talk to someone as soon as possible.

David pulled himself together, finally walking over to me. "Jaz, what happened to the car?"

"I drove it down the highway. It ran out of gas, so I walked off and a truck hit it."

"What?"

"Yes, it was crazy."

"What about the gun?"

"I tossed it in the river four hours away."

"I will tell the police I did all that so your name won't

come up at all; there is no need for both of us to take this blame."

"David, we are going to get you through this. I promise I will never leave your side."

My phone rang and it was the doorman telling me that I had a few guests. I told him it was OK to let them up. I figured it was David's mom and his two sisters wanting to see David's face before he turned himself in.

"I'm going to take a quick shower, baby. Just try to keep my mom calm until I come out the bathroom."

I knew that would be hard because she was furious. David went into the bathroom and I rushed to open the door only to find David's mom and two police officers.

CHAPTER 18

"WHAT THE FUCK, Ms. Bowens?" I said as an officer stepped inside my place without asking. He was very short, shorter than me for sure. He had thick eyebrows and a very shallow mustache. His eyes were scary. I tried to read his name plate but I couldn't make out the name; I just knew it started with a T. I was quickly distracted as the second officer walked in. I noticed how different they were; this officer was a slim white man with slick brown hair. His name plate read *Bryan*.

"Jaz, they were at my house while I was on the phone and said it was better that they pick David up."

"Where is he?" one officer asked.

I sat there, unresponsive, just staring at David's mom. What type of shit was this? What type of mom brings the police to her son? I reached for my phone to try to call the lawyer one more time, but when I looked up, David was coming out the bathroom.

"Get on your knees!" the short officer said while drawing a gun on David.

"Ma, you called the cops?" David asked as he looked his mom in the face.

"Baby, you don't understand," Ms. Bowens pleaded.

"Understand what? You trust these pigs, Ma?"

"Hands up now," the police yelled.

Ms. Bowens started to scream, "Don't shoot him, please don't shoot him!"

"Mom, stop crying," David pleaded.

"Get down now!" the slim white cop screamed.

"Lord, help us. Help my baby, Lord," Ms. Bowens prayed.

"Ma'am, with all due respect, shut up," the white officer said.

"You shut up, muthafucka," David screamed at the officer.

David's mom continued to pray out loud, disregarding what the officer said.

David couldn't take his mother crying, so he started walking toward her. He never got on the ground. His arms were opened wide, his chest still wet from the shower and his bottom covered with a towel. He looked pitiful as he softly said, "It's all right, Mom."

"This is the last time I'm going to tell you get on the ground, boy!" the white cop with dark hair screamed.

David was still walking toward his mom when my phone vibrated loudly on the counter.

Pow pow pow, was all I heard. I jumped and my phone fell from my hand. I looked in the eyes of the short black cop that fired the shot at David and screamed, "Son of a bitch!"

I saw David's body lying on the floor, facedown. First, it looked as if he just tripped over something, but moments later blood started to come from under his body. We were quiet. Ms. Bowens's hand was over her mouth but as soon as the blood started to come from under David's body, she lost it.

She tried to attack the black cop that shot the gun. He immediately drew his gun at her, forcing her to get back. I grabbed her as the slim white cop called in what happened over the radio.

David's mom kneeled down, trying to get closer to David's body, but the Slim Shady-looking cop interfered. "Please, ma'am, step back."

I tried grabbing her arm but she snapped back at me, "You! Goddamn it, *you*! My son didn't have any enemies, so I know this is caused by your problematic ass!"

"What?"

"My baby, Lord, my baby," she yelled.

More cops came rushing to my unit, screaming at me and Ms. Bowens.

"Where is the paramedic?" Ms. Bowens yelled.

"Get back and shut up," one cop yelled back at us.

I couldn't cry or scream, I was so in shock. I sat there on

the floor, looking at my best friend's body lying there. This was all because of me.

Finally, the paramedics walked in with several cops. As one cop propped my door open, I could see other people that lived on my floor trying to peek inside my unit. One paramedic kneeled down to feel if David had a pulse and shook his head at the cops. Ms. Bowens finally stopped screaming and crawled over to David's body, kissing him and rubbing on him. One cop tried to stop her, but the others let her have her way.

I still sat there, staring at the officer who took the shot. I will never forget his face and what he did.

CHAPTER 19

TWO WEEKS LATER, I still couldn't function right. I couldn't attend David's funeral the previous week. I couldn't see him lying in a casket, knowing it was my fault. I hadn't been to the salon at all. I had Miss B shut down the boutique side, and she ran the salon by collecting the booth rent and making sure it was locked down properly.

I had no idea about my life anymore, and most days I wanted to end it. I felt like I had no purpose in living. Every day was a repeated cycle of drugs and alcohol. I finally had a real supplier for pills now. I was so high at times that I could barely think straight, and that's the way I liked it. I was smoking weed, popping pills, and drinking whatever I could most of the day; I couldn't close my eyes because I would only see David rushing to hug his mom and being shot.

"Who is it?" I yelled at the door after hearing a light tap.

TYPICAL CHI SH*T

"Miss B. Open up the door, Jaz."

I crawled to the door because I was so high that I could barely walk.

"Jaz, oh my God. Look at you and look at this place! You are going to the hospital."

"No!" I yelled.

Miss B grabbed my arm and dragged me out my door and down my hall. Before I knew it, she had me in her back seat headed north toward the hospital. I couldn't fight back because I was so high; before we got to the hospital, I started throwing up in the back seat of Miss B's brand new Lexus truck. I couldn't comprehend what she was saying, but it was a lot of curse words. By the time we arrived at the hospital, I was too weak and messy from the vomit so Miss B went inside to get help.

"Please, help my daughter. Her eyes are rolling and she's making weird noises."

I could barely see anything, but I could feel a hand touching under my neck and my arms.

"We barely got a pulse. Get her in a room," I heard someone say.

I couldn't see or feel, but I could hear everything. After five minutes of a lot of rolling, I heard machines for a moment then I heard nothing.

"What time is it?" I said after opening my eyes in a room that was quiet and cold. I looked around and noticed a big clock on the wall that read 6:30. But as dark as the room was, I couldn't make out if it was the morning or the evening. I also noticed other patients in the room sleeping peacefully.

A nurse came over with a cup of water. "Hi, Jaz. I'm your nurse, Mrs. Martin."

"Where am I?"

"You are in recovery. Now that you're awake, I will let your doctor and mom know."

"My mom is here?" I was confused.

"Yes, she's been here all night."

"Are you sure? My mother?"

"Yes. Just try to relax and drink the water. I will get her for you."

The nurse was very nice and soft spoken, but I thought she was a little crazy saying my mom was waiting for me. *Who could she be talking about?* I pondered.

I watched a big circle clock in the room go from 6:30 to 7:30 before someone finally came inside to roll me out to another room. The new room was bigger with only one bed in there.

"Hi, Jaz. I'm Dr. Smith. How do you feel?"

"I'm fine. Can you please tell me what's going on?"

"Yes. You were full of drugs, so we had to pump your stomach. You also had to get a D&C."

"Excuse me?"

"A D&C is a procedure we do to scrape your uterus after a miscarriage."

"Miscarriage? I was pregnant?"

"Yes. It passed through."

I started crying; I had a baby inside me and didn't even know. There was a knock on the door. Before it opened, the doctor said, "This must be your mom. She has been here all night worried sick; she's been making sure we check on you every five minutes."

"My mom?" I asked.

"Come in, she's ready," the doctor said, looking back at the door.

CHAPTER 20

"MISS B," I said after smacking my lips.

"Jaz, I've been worried all night." She rushed over to hug on me.

"I'm going to step out and give you a second," the doctor said.

"My mom?"

"They wouldn't let me ask so many questions if I said I was anybody else. I know you're not that crazy to think your real mom was here?"

I got quiet because yes, I was that crazy.

"I'm so glad you are all right. The doctor said if I didn't bring you when I did, you would be dead."

"What?"

"Yes, Jaz. You are moving in with me so I can watch you for a few months."

I took a deep breath because she was not going to let this go.

"I don't know what you breathing hard for. You need protection."

"Protection from what?" I questioned with my eyebrows raised.

"Britt!"

"Excuse me?"

"Britt has been looking all over for you. She busted out the shop windows, and she's been making social media threats."

"I'm not worried about her, Miss B."

"That little bitch better not let me catch her," Miss B said.

"Ouch."

"What's wrong?"

"My head is hurting bad."

"I'll go get the doctor."

Miss B made a dash out to the doctor, and I could finally breathe. She was taking it too far, saying that I had to move in with her. I was grown and I would handle this just like every other tragedy in my life. My head was starting to hurt; it had felt like a rock was sitting on top of my brain.

"You bitch!" I heard a familiar voice coming from the door. When I looked up, it was Britt standing there with her small round belly sticking out.

"Excuse me? And how did you know I was here?"

"I knew eventually you would try to kill yourself because that's how weak you are."

"Bitch, get out," I said as I reached for the controller to buzz the nurse.

"Bitch, you got my baby daddy killed!" she screamed as she charged toward me, socking me in my face. My arm had an IV needle in it, but that didn't stop me from catching her hair, wrapping it in my hand, and beating her face in. I couldn't feel or see anything. The only thing on my mind was that this bitch just claimed David as her baby's father.

The betrayal of this hoe had me going crazy. There was blood everywhere when I opened my eyes. She was still swinging back, so I reached for the metal remote on the side of the bed and really started to ram it in her face. Blood started shooting in the air. By the time the nurse entered the room, there was blood all over my face and body. Miss B came into the room.

"Jaz, stop it, please!" Miss B's voice was loud and clear.

But a nurse screamed, "Someone call hospital security and police now!"

"We need help for the victim; she's bleeding out," a male voice yelled.

My eyes started to close and I heard so many different voices in the room. I was numb. The doctor gave me a shot of something because I felt a pinch on the top of my arm. I was still hearing chaos and then it got very shallow.

I was blinded by a flashlight as I finally woke up. I looked up and saw a different doctor with the flashlight pen by my face. My mouth was dry as cotton and my eyes felt like they had sand in them. I tried to move my hand to wipe my eyes, but I was handcuffed to the bed.

"What is this?" I screamed.

Two detectives entered the room. One was Detective Williams—the guy that always came to my rescue. I smiled at him, but his face was not the same face I had last seen a few months ago at David's graduation.

"Jaz, you are under arrest for the attempted murder of Brittany Staples."

"What?"

"Yes. You beat her nearly to death yesterday. The doctors sedated you to calm you down."

"I don't understand. She—" I attempted to say she hit me first as if we were kids on a playground, but Detective Williams wouldn't let me speak.

"Jaz, please don't say nothing without a lawyer. Miss B has a lawyer coming here for you."

Tears started to run down my face. *What the fuck did I do?* I only remembered Britt walking into my room with her pregnant belly, hitting me.

"I didn't mean to hurt her," I whispered to myself, but Detective Williams was right by me.

He whispered, "I know, Jaz. You will get through this."

"You have the right to remain silent," the other detective said.

There I was, nineteen years old, with a bank account full of cash and a ready-made business, and I couldn't keep my head on straight. I let drugs, alcohol, and sex ruin me. I couldn't accept the fact that my parents were gone, so I used my pain to hurt everyone around me. I was in deep thought about my life. It felt like a rush, and I really didn't want to live it anymore.

CHAPTER 21

365 DAYS LATER

One year later, I was sitting in my court-appointed AA meeting, about to accept a plaque. I was found not guilty on the attempted murder charge. The judge did charge me with battery and ordered me to get help and stay sober. My lawyer was worth every penny of my twelve thousand dollars.

I was originally let out on a house arrest order that was for six months. Miss B got what she wanted—me at her house—so she could watch me as if I were a kid, and I guess my actions had been immature and stupid.

In the past six months, I was able to start online college classes. I also started my AA judge-appointed class, and it had been interesting. As I sat in my last AA meeting, I couldn't help but smile. It felt good to be clean and have my self-respect back. I had substituted pain for temporary pleasure, and I promised myself never to get that low again. Although some days I got sad thinking of David, I learned through my therapy to exercise and write things out instead of keeping things bottled up inside. I should have gone to therapy right after my mom died instead of going to sex and drugs.

"Jaz Harris," I heard called out from my AA coach, Mrs. Brenda Banks. She had a plaque in her hand. It was a plaque with my name on it that read, "Congratulations! One day at a time has become twelve months of solid recovery."

I proceeded to walk to the front of the room that was filled with much older people who were beat up in the face from all the years of drugs and alcohol. The last twelve months had been different for a girl my age. My AA family helped provide encouragement that got me back on the right track and living my best life. I couldn't help but think about how crazy it was the way life had taken its turn on me.

I felt as though this was the high school diploma I never got. I smiled the biggest smile, and my head was held high as I made my way to the front, dressed in white jeans and a white blouse. Pink pedicured toes peeked out from my wedge heels; they matched my pink manicure. The day that filled me with pain a year ago was turning out to be a good day.

"Yay! Jazzy! You did it!" my group chanted.

The class clapped and cheered, yelling, "Jazzy! Go, Jazzy!" as I walked past.

Jazzy was the name given to me by an older family

member I had shared a story about. That had been my name since. They said the name fit me well because on the first day I walked in the meeting dressed to perfection. I didn't wear a full face of makeup, but I always had on some lip gloss and lashes. Having myself together was essential because it was all for Mr. James "Boxer" Jones.

James Jones was the meeting coordinator, who also happened to be the owner of the building. He was six foot five, around two hundred fifty pounds solid, and a boxer. James had a bald head with a full beard, and he always wore a White Sox fitted cap. He had the pinkest lips. I mean, the lips that any girl would just look at and want to kiss. I sure did. Every time we talked, I could never focus on what he was saying because I was looking at his juicy lips and perfect white teeth.

One part of this building had a boxing gym for youth to practice boxing. He helped a lot of kids and young adults as well. James sure saved my life with those AA meetings. The counseling helped me to stop drinking, but the relationships I'd built with the other addicts were much needed. The path I was on caused me to lose my friends, my family, and almost my life.

"Congrats, Jazzy," a voice behind me said.

I turned around and it was that pink-lipped, tall, handsome James.

"Thank you, Mr. Boss Man," I replied, never taking my eyes off his mouth.

"Now that you are done with this program, I have an offer for you."

Sure, baby. Anything for you if it includes a kiss. Of course, that's what I was thinking.

"What do you need me to do?" I said as I ignored my thoughts.

"I have a group of high school freshman girls that come every week, and I usually have a motivational speaker teach them self-esteem and the dos and don'ts of life. I wanted you to speak to them for a few weeks. It would be nice to have your face around here for a little longer."

I dropped my plaque on the ground and we almost bumped heads trying to pick it up at the same time.

"I don't want to pressure you, Jaz. I just think you have a unique story and your story could probably save another teen's life. Plus, I will compensate you for your time," James said, trying to make me feel good about being nineteen years old and completing a twelve-month Alcoholics Anonymous class.

"I don't know, James. Those girls need a real speaker. I'm not the one."

"Jaz, you came into this program and kept your head high. You are twelve months clean, and I can look at you and tell that you have a made a full recovery. Let your story light up another girl's future."

James was persistent and, as much as I wanted to run full speed out the door, I couldn't help but wonder if my story could actually help another girl. I sure wished I had help months ago. The people that I thought were helping me were using me for sex, fun, and money. The people I trusted with my life were lying to my face. The betrayal of friends took me on an emotional roller coaster that caused me to use a good friend.

"Is that a yes, Jaz?"

"Yes, I'll do it."

"Well, the girls are wrapping up a session now if you want to go introduce yourself. Just walk over to the next room," James said with the biggest smile.

It felt like James was flirting with me, and Lord knows he was sexy as fuck. But along with my sobriety, I was also practicing celibacy.

As I got in the room, there were twelve girls of all different sizes. James said they were eighth graders, but these girls looked as old as I was. Their nails were long and studded, and they had over twenty-four inches of weave. Their lashes had to be blinding them because I couldn't see an eyeball. I felt more nervous than ever now, looking at these grown-ass little girls. They were surely going to judge my alcoholic ass.

The room grew quiet as I stood in front of a group of girls that looked older than me, waiting to hear my advice on being a good high school student when my own story was the worst.

The room was quiet, the girls were on their phone, and suddenly one girl that was sitting in the front looked me dead in my face.

"Is that an AA key chain hanging on your purse? My old-ass aunties carry a bunch of them around."

"Language!" one of the female teachers shouted from the back of the room.

"Sorry," the dirty-ass teenage girl said.

"Please respect Jaz. She will be giving you girls some encouragement these next few weeks," James said as he placed one arm on my shoulder, nudging me to speak up.

At this point, it was get to talking or be prepared for these kids to say more stuff that I didn't like. I didn't know what to say, so I looked on the back of my plaque and read it out loud.

"Twelve months. Fifty-two weeks. Three hundred sixty-five days. That's how long it's been since I had a drink or popped a pill."

"Wow, you're so beautiful," one girl from the back of the room blurted.

"What's wrong with having a lil' sippy sip?" the loud, dirty girl from the front of the room said while laughing again.

I stared at her with her black crop top, black dusty-ass leggings, and black Air Force 1s on. I could tell she was about to be a problem. Anybody wearing black Air Force 1s wanted all the smoke, but she met her match. We had a five-year age difference, and I was only recovering from drinking, not from slapping the shit out of bitches—including baby bitches.

"I don't mean to be nosy, but you are so pretty and look

as young as us. How did you become addicted to alcohol and pills?" the pretty girl in the back asked. The name *Isis* hung on a chain around her neck.

As the big black-shoed girl smacked her lips, I pulled a chair close to me and took a seat. I knew this was about to take a while. Just maybe my story could help her because she had destruction written all over her face. This was going to be a challenge, but I was sure my therapist would be happy to know I had something lined up like this.

"Well, I guess we are stuck together for a few weeks," I stated as I walked out the door.

"I owe you big time," James said once we entered the hall.

"You sure do. Especially if I don't slap one of them hot lil' girls."

He laughed right before giving me the tightest hug. Damn, he smelled so good. I mean, everything about James was perfect and I didn't know how long this celibacy would last if he kept giving me hugs.

"OK, see you next week," he said.

"Yes. Thank you for the opportunity."

Today had been perfect—the most normal day I'd had in a while. I felt like I really made a positive step in my life and it took a while to get to this point. This had been a life-learning rush for me, and now I was on a mission to teach younger girls to keep pushing when times got hard. And I was on a personal mission to get Mr. James Jones.

"James and Jaz," I sang as I walked to my car, clicking my heels.

About the Author

WRITING WAS SASSY Silverman's outlet as a child. Instead of standing up to her bully, she'd go home and write about what she should've done and what would happen the next time she saw her. But every time she saw her bully, she froze. Her sixth-grade teacher found her notebook and read it. She said, "These plays you're writing are well thought out." Sassy was confused because she thought some of the words she'd used would get her into big trouble. Her teacher told all the other teachers how good of a writer Sassy was and applauded her for something she thought was wrong. Her teacher wanted her to find someone with whom to act out the plays in front of the class. She did, and afterwards, she was no longer afraid to confront her bully.

Sassy continued to express her feelings on paper. She decided to write every day because it felt good. Writing helped her overcome bullying and many more dilemmas she faced growing up. Writing was her safe place. She fell in love with urban fiction after reading *The Coldest Winter Ever* by Sister Souljah. And she fell even deeper after reading *Push* by

Sapphire. These two urban classics inspired Sassy Silverman to write more as a child. Writing feeds her soul, and after so many years of burying her stories, she's finally at a place where she wants to share her creativity with the world.

"I once read a quote by Mark Twain: 'The two most important days in your life are the day you are born and the day you find out why.' Well today, I found out that I'm meant to be a writer."

—*Sassy Silverman*

Thank you for reading *Typical Chi Sh*t*.
If you enjoyed this book, please help spread
the word by leaving an online review.

KEEP IN TOUCH WITH SASSY SILVERMAN

Facebook: SweetSassy Silverman

Instagram: @_worldofsass

Made in the USA
Monee, IL
04 March 2025

13456316R00090